ADAM BENDER

The characters and events portrayed in this book are fictitious. Any similarity to real persons, living or dead, is coincidental and not intended by the author.

This novel is for my parents, who let me play with the typewriter and encouraged me to write.

CONTENTS

1
AWAKE

The light is blinding. I shake off the sweat in a shiver. A million needles stab, and something is hammering and pounding away above me. I roll into the cool shadow of a towering tree.

Stop. It's just a nightmare. I'm still in bed; just need to open my eyes. Just get them open and this will all be over.

My neck itches—a tick, maybe. I picture the insect's dark head sinking into my skin, its abdomen ballooning red. I sit up fast, scratching all the way. As I gasp for air, my eyes absorb row after row of gray wood.

I thrash about, a futile attempt to improve the reception. Nothing makes sense; all I get is static and a strengthened headache. The woodpecker hacks away.

Oh my God—it's not a dream. I'm in a forest.

I close my eyes and let a warm breeze brush through my hair.

"Think, damn it," I breathe at last. "How did you get here?"

My clothes are damp and feature spots of mud, but nothing is torn. Stranger still, my body aches, but my skin shows no signs of cuts or even bruising. It's like I just up and decided to spend a night in the woods—but forgot the tent and sleeping bag. Was I drunk? I can't remember anything about last night.

Frantically, I search my pockets. No wallet, no keys, no cell phone… only thing in there is a crumpled-up brochure.

"You have to be kidding me," I groan, tossing it on the grass.

Unless…

I snap up the ball of paper, carefully unfurl it. Emblazoned across the top are miracle words: *National Park Visitor's Map*. Better, someone's drawn two circles with a marker—one around the end marker of a trail and the other around a station labeled *MONORAIL*. I must have used the map to get here. But why?

Sitting isn't doing me any good, and the headache's starting to subside, anyway. I'm sure things will come together as soon as I get home—if I can find it.

Shut up, you couldn't have honestly forgotten—

No, I didn't forget. I couldn't have. I'm just disoriented still. This is what happens when you sleep outside on the grass all night. I don't know what hallucinogen I did last night before coming here, but I'm never doing it again.

Okay, so where's the trail?

I stare into the wilderness. Could I actually have taken a trail to get here? Was I too wasted to remember anything, but sober enough to stick to a path?

Wait. Is that—?

The tree on the other end of the clearing—something's scratched into its trunk. I stagger to my feet and limp the rest of the way. My socks squish.

Graffiti—some idiot decided to take a pocketknife and carve the numeral 7. The whole thing is senseless and illogical, but it confirms civilization is nearby. I squint into the vegetation and pan slowly, left to right. My eyes land on a path—overgrown with weeds, but a path nonetheless.

●

The density of green is overwhelming. And the birds—the damn birds are everywhere, all singing for mates. Too bad I'm not here on a hiking trip.

What the hell is wrong with me? I'm lost in the woods, don't have the slightest idea why, and what do I do? Make jokes! Make stupid jokes! If I'd just focus, I might be out of this mess already.

●

A new sound: trickling water. I dash for the source and almost run right through a stream. Splashing and guzzling ensues.

The ripples fade. I don't recognize the youthful eyes staring back at me, but a touch confirms the gaping mouth and patchy beard are my own.

The bushes on the other side of the stream rustle and snap, and two large deer tiptoe out into the open. They stare at me, bodies frozen stiff. I take one more hit of the cool liquid and rise to my feet. "Enjoy," I say with a wave toward the water. The doe, apparently alarmed by my suggestion, turns around and bolts back into the shrubbery. The buck continues to stare.

I force a grin. He runs after her.

Oh God—now I'm talking to animals. If I don't find humans soon I'm probably going to end up completely insane. But all I can see is the green and all I can hear are the birds. Who's to say I actually woke up in the place circled on the map? I could be anywhere. Is this really even a trail?

Shut up. Keep going. Follow the trail.

•

Winged insects hiss in my ear and bite my arms and face, apparently attracted to my sweat and extreme body odor. The further into the vegetation I push, the more the bugs seem to attack, the more they foil my pitiable attempts to distract myself from the present.

This is insane. I don't know where I am, I don't know how I got here... I don't even recognize my own face!

I can't afford to rest, though. I have to keep going until I find somewhere I can get help and sort things out. I'll be okay if I just keep moving.

Maybe I shouldn't have got going so fast—should've looked around where I woke a few minutes more. I might have found some answers right there. God, why didn't I think of that? Maybe I should turn back.

No, right now, all that's important is survival. I should probably call it a miracle I woke up at all. I might have been on the brink of death. And if that's true, I'm not going to waste a second chance at life scrounging around for hints to my past. That's like—I don't know—selfish or something. Screw that.

This is way too much like a dream. Why can't I just open my eyes?

•

My eyes lift to the horizon and swerve nearly 90 degrees with the path. It turns away from a strange blue patch of light—a surreal end of the forest. Curious, I drift off the beaten trail and through the thin layer of trees.

The cliff drops more feet than I have time to estimate, but below and far beyond is a shore-side metropolis. The skyscrapers and white-speckled ocean are as familiar as déjà vu, but I can't attach a name to the picture. My eyes ride an ivory-toned structure from the city edge back to a large, tin-roofed building about a mile below.

The monorail station. The map was right.

•

I return to the trail, trot along it with renewed energy. The path slopes down the mountainside. I glance up at the sun to get an idea of the time, but dark clouds have invaded the sky.

My mind replays the awakening, the futile scan for meaning. I scream wildly. A bird returns the cry.

Calm down, damn it. Take things one step at a time. Just make it to the city and the haze will clear. You're hungry and aching—of course you can't think straight. Of course you can't—

My surroundings snap me back into the present like a well-timed slap to the face. The path has opened up into a field—no, a cemetery. Cold fog seethes around the graves and down my spine. The stones all have the same stark contour, but they've chipped individually with age. A granite soldier watches over them, a menacing hawk perched on one outstretched arm. Below his boots are words: *These soldiers gave their lives for Unity. They will be remembered for Heroism in a time of Great Civil Strife.*

I glance upwards, freeze under the hawk's icy stare.

The train station can't be far. This is a graveyard; there's got to be at least a parking lot nearby. If I can find that, I can find the train.

I pick a random direction and move on. Every advance through the white curtain reveals another hundred tombstones, and the taste of stale death comes with each breath. It's irritatingly quiet—even the birds have shut up. I need to get out of here.

I'm running. My ankle screams, the world blurs, and I'm face-first in the dirt, caught in death's shadow. Something cold licks my neck—my eyes bolt skyward and watch several hundred liquid daggers scream into my face. I scramble to my feet and sprint through another marble row.

The storm grows torrential, and the rain's static drone amplifies my lungs' wheezing. My legs give out just as I reach a crumbling flight of stairs and a war-torn chapel—shelter. I keel over and spit thick yellow mucus into the grass.

•

The chapel's rotten doors are two times my height and at least ten times my age. I push hard and tumble through. The fall sets fire to my arms and legs, pierces them with jagged shards of red and yellow. The windows blew out long ago—all the color's dropped to the rock floor. I clench my teeth and tug at the glass.

The old church smells of mildew and I can see why: without glass, the rain comes through the windows in buckets. I lumber down an aisle that zigzags between twenty-or-so off-kilter pews, and find a seat somewhere the middle that's as far from the water as I can get.

God—what happened to this place?

I pull out the map and trace my path to the cemetery with a spare finger. The monorail isn't far. As I figured, there's a parking lot nearby, and the train station looks like a quick jaunt from there.

The glossy paper reflects a blinding lightning flash into my eyes. Stupid storm. Why did this have to happen now? Dramatic effect?

Suddenly, my right sock is wet and sticky.

Oh, my ankle's bleeding. Great. Must have cut it when I fell down. Probably aren't any tissues in here.

I bend over, use my hand to press my pant leg against the wound. Hope this helps.

It doesn't make sense. None of this makes sense.

I tug at the map and scan it for any additional information

about my whereabouts. But there's nothing—just a big forest called National Park.

My stomach rumbles. When was the last time I ate? The pain seems to intensify the more I focus on it, and the more I ache, the more attention I seem to allow. I can feel acid in the back of my throat, demanding.

"You know what?" I say aloud for whatever reason. The train station is probably sheltered, too. There's no point wasting more time here. Anyway, I'm already wet and gross. I'll get myself cleaned up when I make it to the city.

A peculiar quiet takes hold of the church the second I stand up. I glance up at the window. The storm is over—or at least slowing down for the time being.

"Please, don't start up again," I pray as I reach the stairs back into the graveyard. There's still a sprinkle, but it's a vast improvement from five minutes ago.

My ankle burns with every step, but I grit my teeth and limp through the graves like a zombie. Several hundred tombstones later, I find more cracked marble steps. They descend into a parking lot.

•

I scratch at a red mosquito bite. Too bad I didn't wake up next to a can of repellant.

The lot is empty, but a large yellow sign with the word MONORAIL and an arrow gives me direction. One marker leads to another. This one's vandalized with the word SUCKS, sprayed in red over a crossed-out RAIL. Once I get over the cleverness of it all, I continue on through a giant, grass-covered metal pipe. I plod into the dark and dank passageway; it twists a few times before finally opening into light.

The monorail station stabs through the pastoral beauty of the land. Only the unkempt ivy twisting over its dark metal surface keep the structure rooted in the forest. Jet black stairs climb from the earth into the blue sky just beyond, but their entrance is gated and watched by a blank-faced man standing erect in navy blue uniform.

"Good afternoon," he greets. "Put your arms in the air."

I follow his advice and he starts patting down my shirt.

"You don't look well. Why are your clothes torn?"

"I tripped, fell through some bushes."

"You're early. The train won't be here for another two hours."

"I didn't have a choice."

He stares me cold in the eyes, calculating. Then with a quick turn he pulls open the gate.

The steps clank under my feet and the wind whistles loud in my ears. A whirring camera attached to the overhang meets me at the top and then swivels away. The station is as empty as the parking lot. The only sign of life comes from some stenciled graffiti on the wall, an eerily realistic jet black silhouette of a man with fiery red eyes.

I slump against the wall and gaze vacantly at a tight entanglement of trees just beyond the tracks. I'm awake.

2
MONORAIL

A clean-cut and pot-bellied old man steps onto the platform—the first person to arrive in the near two hours I've been waiting. He walks by, takes a seat a few benches away and begins eyeing his wristwatch.

A soft hum grows into an angry, mechanical roar. For an instant the silver bullet seems to move in slow motion. The wind rushes through my hair, and I take a step back as the train hurtles into the station.

"If you see someone leave a bag," an automated voice is saying, "kindly ask them, 'Is that your bag?' If it's not theirs, please alert the station security center immediately. We value your help in keeping Monorail safe."

The steel doors slide apart. "Welcome," it says.

•

The monorail is obsessively clean; oversized modular windows provide the only color. Thankfully, the car is half-filled with people. The man who'd waited an astounding 30 seconds for the train to come takes a seat adjacent to mine. The doors snap shut, and a bored-looking fellow in a conductor's hat shifts through the car.

Shit! The whole concept of paying for public transportation somehow slipped my mind. I frantically search my pockets for money but come up empty.

The pudgy old man next to me is staring. "Are you broke, son?" he asks.

"I...uh, I could have sworn I had—"

"Don't worry about it," he says with a wave of the hand. "I'll cover you."

"Thank you—I'm really sorry to make you—"

"No worries, happened to me the other day," he laughs. "What's your name?"

My name... Oh my God, I can't even remember my name. I cycle through all that's left of my memory, search for anything that sounds even remotely usable. What was that graffiti I saw? On that tree—it was a number. What was it?

"Seven," I say. The announcement takes me by surprise. "Um, yeah, call me Seven." Great, I just named myself after tree graffiti. Well done, man, well done.

"I'm George." He drops a handful of loose change into the conductor's hands. "This is for my friend here," he explains with a nerve-wracking grin.

"Thanks again," I say weakly.

"You're lucky I was sitting here. Most people these days are too paranoid to loan money to a perfect stranger...let alone one as ragged-lookin' as yourself."

"Heh...thanks." My eyes lower to the floor. How many times am I gonna have to thank this guy?

I gaze up at one of the many advertisements lining the space above the windows. This one isn't so much a promotion. It reads in big block letters: *PATRIOTS ARE THE TRUE. HERETICS ARE THE DAMNED.*

"Visiting the cemetery, eh?" George asks me, still beaming like a saint.

"Yeah, it's quite..."

"Magnificent, isn't it?" George interrupts. "I have some old friends buried out there—gave their lives in that Great War. If it weren't for them, we'd still be overrun with Heretics."

An elaboration on that would be helpful, of course, but I don't want to sound like an utter moron and ask about a war everyone seems to think is so goddamned great. I nod instead, but he still takes it as a cue to continue.

"My unit actually fought near that cemetery. Of course, it was just a big field at the time. I think there were more trees, too. Anywho, the government had just discovered the rebels' center of operations was deep in those woods. We were one of the troops that got sent in to take it down. Victory was in our reach! Oh, what a feeling! Have you ever thought about joining the Guard?"

"It's crossed my mind," I say.

"I loved every minute of it—retired last year. I was eventually promoted to lieutenant!" George's eyes light up. "But where was I?"

"Victory was in your reach."

"Ah yes, victory in our very grasp! What a rush of adrenaline! Made us a bit cocky, I s'pose—we were so noisy in those woods. The rebels suddenly appeared and opened fire before we even got to their base! I dived behind a large boulder for cover—threw a grenade into the blaze! It was bloody—like nothing you've ever seen—but for such a noble cause!"

"Right."

"'If you're going to keep your house tidy, you have to eliminate the termites'—that's what my mother would always say. I'll never forget that!"

George's mood shifts to gloomy. "Jimmy didn't make it—shot between the eyes—nothing we could do. He wouldn't see the nation reunited. I dedicated every kill at the rebel base to that brave soul!" He swallows. "But what an adventure! What an absolutely exceptional—"

"So how long does it take the train to get to the city?"

"You're not from around here, eh?"

"I'm on vacation."

"Oh, how interesting!" he says. "Where do you hail from?"

Eventually, I decide I hail from "a small town up north."

"Oh, I have some buddies up in Loganville," George gushes. "Bob and Johnny! They fought beside me you know! They have some incredible war tales of their own, let me tell you! Why, Johnny, he took out an entire camp all on his lonesome. He was an explosives expert, see."

"Ah," I smile weakly.

"I'm sorry, I haven't even answered your question yet, have I, my boy? We should be there within the hour."

I frown.

"Didn't you bring a book?"

I woke up in the middle of a fucking forest! "Uh no, I left it behind by mistake." I wish I didn't have to be so dishonest with a guy his age. I just really don't want this conversation to get any more complex than it needs to.

"Shame, that. I've got a magazine if you'd like."

"Oh, that would be great, thanks." Dammit, that's the fourth time I've thanked him. Good thing he's handing me a reason to disengage.

The magazine is labeled *National News Weekly*. Emblazoned on its cover is a photograph of a fit, middle-aged man in soldier garb saluting and smiling intriguingly at something just above my head. A large caption below his neck reads *President Drake, Poised For Greatness!*

Perplexed, I glance at George, who's smiling a bit stupidly at the landscape outside the train window. My eyes shift back to the magazine while my fingers flip to the cover story, *Leading Our Powerful Nation*. The article is a Q&A, composed more of big glossy pictures than text.

There's not much in the way of an introduction, and I cringe at the first question:

Q. How are things going overall?

I get the feeling this isn't going to be that hard-hitting of a story, and I'm right. Question after question demands information on the health and happiness of Drake's family. Apparently, they're all *just dandy*, as the President describes it. Drake likes to call his wife Betty his *extra leg*. His daughter Sarah is about to graduate high school and plans to attend the President's alma mater, National University. His son Tom just made the honor roll for the fourth straight semester at National.

I wonder if Drake's offspring are actually smart. Wouldn't there be some incentive to pass the President's kids with flying colors? Not to be cynical or anything—it's not like I'm from around here.

Q. How are you feeling as President?

What kind of ridiculous, open-ended question is that? Maybe the reason Drake's son is doing so well is just that college professors in this country suck.

Drake: Nothing could be better! The nation is the strongest it's been in years. And it was already the most powerful in the world, so I think we're doing pretty well. I'll be the first to admit that being elected President is somewhat intimidating at first, but I've attacked that beast and now the role and its responsibilities are really just a natural extension of my life.

Despite the bold Q preceding it, the next question isn't actually a question.

Q. The economy is booming.

Drake: The economy is stronger than it's ever been! The great thing about this fine nation is that with a little work, anyone can accomplish their life dreams. A colleague of mine commented to me yesterday that our nation is at its peak, the best it's ever been. I disagree. We will never be at our peak. Let us all keep working to be all that we can be.

The subject turns to war—one's going on, I guess. Drake tells the reporter that progress is being made and that the stage we're at right now is exactly where we should be.

Q. How is the Heretic situation at home?

Drake: It's not a situation.

George clears his throat. "Good news, eh?" he articulates so matter-of-factly it sounds more like a declaration than a question.

I pause long. "Yeah."

"This is the finest nation in the world!" the old man gushes.

I smile politely, lean back in my seat, and gaze again at the *PATRIOTS ARE THE TRUE. HERETICS ARE THE DAMNED* poster. Three indigo trucks slide by my window. Golden hawk emblems are plastered to their sides.

Still eyeing the magazine over my shoulder, George

enthusiastically declares, "Damn them Heretics!" He clenches his teeth and shakes his fist.

I nod silently and flip to another article.

Learning about the President's apparently superb taste for fine wine gets old fast, so I put the periodical down. I slouch a bit more in my chair and lay my head back against the scratched plastic window. Too bad I got so much sleep last night.

Across the way, a little girl holding a pink, heart-shaped pillow leans against her mother's side. Both wear headphones, their eyes fixed upon a tiny screen on the mother's lap. The girl's eyes are wide, the mother's half-closed.

I swivel to the window again and watch fields of corn fly by. What will I do when I get into the city? Finding answers is easier said than done. Without memory I have nowhere to go, no one I can contact.

●

"Will you look at that," George says admiringly. My eyes unglaze and follow his finger out the window. A barn in the distance is enveloped in flames. Dark clouds of smoke billow out. of the top. A pair of men in midnight blue uniforms stand with rifles relaxed at their sides, smirking at the burning structure.

"What the hell? Why are they just standing there?" I scan the area for a fire engine, an ambulance, something…

"Must be one of them damn rebel groups hiding out in there," he says, grinning.

"The soldiers set it on fire?" I sputter back.

The question appears to irritate George. "The Guard keeps us united," he says. "If we can't stand together, the Heretics have already won."

A figure dressed in black rushes out of the barn. His arms stretch into the air.

One soldier lifts a rifle to his shoulder.

Not totally believing, I glance at George. The old man nods his head in approval.

3
THE CITY

A bland urban blur of concrete and steel invades my window.

"No, no, yeah," a pasty teen a few seats over stammers to his portly chum. "I mean, I don't doubt for a second that life began on this planet. It's just that, well, it seems to me that like, I mean, wouldn't it be irrational to assume there isn't life anywhere else?"

"You're an idiot," says his squeaky-voiced compatriot.

"If you'll just hear me out..."

"Hear you out? I've been listening to your sci-fi bullshit for the last twenty minutes!"

"It's not bullshit! I've read stuff about this on the Internet!"

"I've read stuff about your mom on the Internet."

"You have not!"

"Yeah man, she's all over the Web."

"Yeah? Well your mom is all over my—"

"My mom is dead."

Silence. "I meant—I meant your step-mom is..."

I close my eyes in a vain attempt to shut out the chatter. But it only makes the execution replay in my head. "Keeping us united," I mumble.

The engine fades. The buildings focus and slow.

"Do you have a place to stay?" George asks with sudden alarm.

I pretend not to hear him and instead focus on the doors. They don't budge.

"Seven?"

Dammit. "Sorry?"

"Do you have a place to stay?" he says again.

I pause. "Not exactly."

George rips a page of the magazine and pulls a pen out of his pocket. "My sister Claire runs a small youth hostel in the city. I'll write down the address for you. She'll give you a bed if you mention my name."

A youth hostel? Well, that would better than another night in the woods. "Thanks," I reply, shoving the scrap into my pocket.

"You're going to need some cab fare in the meantime," he continues.

Who does this guy think he is? "I don't want to—"

"I'm far from penniless, young man," George says, pulling out a couple paper bills. Both are splashed with the number 20. "Take this."

I hesitate.

"It's okay. They tell me I'm supposed to get rid of money so my family doesn't get taxed when I... well... later on," George says, pushing the money into my hands. "I swear to you, my boy. You'll be doing me a favor."

My fingers close around the green. "Heh," I manage. "Thanks."

The doors slide open. Finally. "Have a good one," I tell George.

I let another hurried passenger clear a path through the crowd and onto an escalator. George is far behind by the time I descend into a fluorescent-lit corridor. The stores sell magazines and cigarettes.

The sparkling sound of a flute fills the air and calms my nerves. My eyes find the source: an old beggar, slouched against the wall. Wish I had some coins—can't afford to give away a twenty.

I walk by. Just ahead is the exit. Orange sunlight streams through scuffed glass.

A deep groan and ringing clatter spins me around. The music's done. The beggar's old instrument case lies upside down against the wall and coins are scattered everywhere. He whimpers, fading in the shadow of a man with *GUARD* sewn onto his blue jacket.

The soldier is rabid.

"You Heretic piece of shit! You can't play that song!"

The drifter holds the flute tight against his heart. "Please."

But the soldier tears the instrument away and lifts it high over his head. It whistles on the way down. Then it cracks in half over the howling musician's neck.

"You'll learn, traitor!" the enforcer barks, pushing the two splintered ends into the beggar's face.

Suddenly, the lizard's eyes slide back in my direction. "What in God's name are you looking at?!"

My head spins like a top; I'm the only one who actually stopped to watch the maniacal violence transpire. I turn, walk fast to the station exit and tear at the door.

•

The warm air comes in hurried gulps. I get a good taste of grilling hot dogs and car exhaust in the process. The avenue is thick with sluggish automobiles and snaking motorcycles. Every few seconds a car horn breaks through the din.

"God damn! What is your problem?!" sneers a man in a leisure suit, walking in my direction.

"Huh?" I make out.

"Susan, for fuck's sake, stop worrying about the fucking dog! He'll be fine!" There's black plastic in his ear—the guy's just on a cell phone. "Look, I just got off work. I'll be home in an hour."

A yellow cab on my side of the street futilely tries to pick up speed by switching to the lane closer to the sidewalk. I wave with one hand, reach into my pocket and crinkle the magazine scrap with the other.

I read him the address. He says something in incoherent, broken English. I smile, nod, and ease myself into the backseat.

"Paper!" He beckons me, so I hand the piece over. He gives it a good, contemplative stare—like it was some kind of word search—and then throws it back at me. The taxi lurches back into the slow traffic.

"Move sopping wet car, shitty fuck for brains!" he yells out his half-rolled window. Then he half-turns to me and laughs, "These fools make me wish I had my dog and my gun."

23

I choke out a laugh. Weird.

The city is surprisingly clean. There must be at least three trash cans per block, and the streets and sidewalks look like they've been recently scrubbed. The building designs are equally unexciting. On the surface, nothing appears to have much historical value, and many of the buildings seem to follow the same design.

The radio snaps on and a tweedy, nasal male voice enters the cab. "—lo Arthur, welcome."

"Thank you for having me, Ian."

"And welcome also to Jimmy."

"Good to be back, Mr. Gambit."

"Good to have you again," declares the host. "Now I want to tackle a different side of the Heretic situation. Is the Guard focusing too much of its energy on the war? Should we perhaps be more worried about Heretics within our own borders? Arthur, let's start with you."

"Well, Ian, to be honest, I don't think we're worrying nearly enough about the Enemy. We've been at war for two years now and—"

"Jimmy?" Ian Gambit interrupts.

"I disagree," he says. "Our nation is just too darn powerful to need to worry about those dang skeeter bugs as much as we worry about 'em. If there's any problem, it's internal."

"So you're saying the larger problem is inside our country."

"Yes, Ian, it's them we need to work on! We need to spend more time hunting the traitors down and bringing them fools to justice!"

"Can I interject?" asks Arthur.

"Go," allows Ian.

"I agree that dissension is a growing problem, but I just think we're already spending too much of our resources on something not nearly as dangerous as—"

"That's a load of crap!" bursts Jimmy. "The Guard is far too strong! We can never be defeated! The only thing that can bring us down is our very own selves. Yes sir, it will be another Great War that destroys this powerful na—"

"That's exactly the attitude that will lead to our annihilation! We think we're invincible, when in reality—"

"Arthur, if I may ask you," says Ian. "Exactly what are you basing your argument on?"

"Well for one thing, the Enemy still has nuclear weapons somewhere!"

"Oh please," laughs Jimmy. "Even if that's true, they wouldn't have the slightest idea what to do with them."

"And what are you basing that argument off of?!"

"Now, calm down, Arthur. Take a deep breath," says Ian.

"I am calm! I—"

"We'll be right back."

"You're listening to 'Backtalk with Ian Gambit,'" oozes a sexed-up female.

"So!" the cabbie suddenly exclaims. "What do you think the President Drake will have to say tonight?"

"Uh, that things are fine?" I reply vaguely.

"He'll have more to say than this, I am certain!" he shouts. "I believe the President Drake has Heresy solution! Are your hands wet, my friend?"

"What?"

"I was driving today at 6 a.m. on 611 with a man and his soggy daughter! My dog likes women, so I carry a gun!"

"Okay?"

We pass by a large glass display of mannequins dressed in flowery skirts and bikini tops. Sweaty shoppers rush around the sidewalks, clinging to large plastic sacks. One woman drops her bag during a frantic rush for her cell phone and starts squawking. A disapproving mother clamps her hands over her son's ears and curses back.

The road curves slightly and a towering chrome building rises into view. I let out an audible gasp. "Cap-toll-ter," the driver comments.

"Excuse me?"

"Capitol Tower! This is first visit, yes?"

"Yes."

"President Drake...he works in that building over there, that one right there. Whole government, very good, very wet!"

"Oh, very good." Nice one, that wasn't an awkward reply at all. Talking to this guy is hurting my vocabulary.

"Monument Park is down this street," the driver waves vaguely out his window.

"Okay."

Sagging back into soft leather, I start worrying about my financial situation. I can't depend on people donating me money. "Hey," I get the driver's attention, "How's the economy, lately?"

"Very good!" he raves. "Praise to President Drake! He keeps things very wet!"

I think I feel the onset of a headache. "So how hard do you think it would be to find a job?"

"Very good! Land of opportunity, they say!" he yells back at me. "But you'll have to take off your pants."

"My pants?!" I nearly bang my head into the padded ceiling.

"Your pants and shirt—not wet! No one will hire unless you carry a gun!" He laughs.

"What?!"

"Not wet! Your shirt! Your pants! Ripped up!"

I slouch back into my original position and exhale.

He's not the first guy to comment on my attire, and he's got a point, even if he is a loon. I've got torn, dirty and probably blood-stained clothing on—not exactly a fashionable style in most places.

Shit. That means I'm going to have to buy something new to wear. There's more money down the drain—do I even have enough for that? Fuck, this guy better not charge me too much for the ride. Hell, I don't even know how much this hostel is going to put me back—hopefully George's name will get me some kind of major discount. Damn it.

The driver turns down a small, residential street, cruises a few blocks and takes another right. Finally, he comes to a stop in front of an old two-floor brick house. A sign on the front reads *Youth Home*.

"Thanks," I say.

He yawns.

"How much?" I ask finally.

"Nineteen-fifty, sir."

You have to be fucking kidding me! This isn't very wet at all! I give him one of my twenties and tell him to keep the change. Not much of a tip, but I'm so fucking broke. He mutters something in a tongue I can't place.

I trudge along the short brick pathway to the hostel entrance, shaking my head. I straighten my oily hair, compose myself, and ring the doorbell. Instead of a traditional "ding-dong," it plays a familiar yet ultimately unidentifiable electronic tune. The door opens and a woman that looks about George's age takes me in with an awkward gasp. Her gray hair is tied tightly in a bun, and her large eyes stare uncertainly. She sniffs the air and frowns slightly.

"Hi," I say. "Are you Claire?"

She nods, but the confusion on her face remains. "Uh," I continue, "I just came in on the Monorail a little while ago and I was talking to your brother, George. I don't have a place to stay and he recommended—"

"Are you Seven?"

"Yeah, I, uh, how did you—?"

"George called me a little while ago; told me to expect a new resident—though I didn't expect you to be so filthy,"

"I'm sorry, I just—"

"Well, aren't you a gentleman!" she smiles. "No need for explanation, come on in."

●

"Have a seat, Seven," says Claire, waving me toward the dining room. "I've got to get a pen and some paper."

The place is nothing fancy but it's got a homey atmosphere. Eight old wooden chairs surround a mahogany table. I slide my hand lightly over its smooth surface before easing into the chair closest to me. This is a hell of a lot better than I expected.

A fat, orange tabby moseys into the room. It pauses to give me a look. I drop my hand low to the carpet and the cat strides over to smell it.

"All right, Seven," Claire says softly as she enters the room.

She's got a blue ballpoint and a yellow pad. "How long will you be staying?"

"I'm, uh....I'm not really sure, actually."

"Well I already have one permanent resident," she says, sitting. "I can't take on another."

I rush a guess. "It shouldn't be any more than a few weeks, I would think."

"Oh I'm just joking, darling! You can stay as long as you need to. I was referring to my grandson, Adrian. He's about your age. Lived here in one of my rooms since..." Claire trails off as her eyes lower to the table. "Well, I guess it's not that important," she mutters. Her eyes flash back to me and she whispers, "Now, George told me you didn't have a lot of money."

"Well...no, not really."

"It's usually twenty a night, but because you're a friend of George I'll bring it down to fifteen. You can pay me later, when you get some money together."

"Thank you...that would really help." Shit, I need a job. "Uh, do you know where I might find a job around here?"

She breathes out sharply, and scrutinizes the carpet for a few seconds. "Well, my grandson works at a bookstore, maybe he can help get you some work there. He's out practicing with his band right now, but maybe you can talk to him tomorrow morning. Oh! That reminds me! Breakfast is complimentary every morning at nine."

"Great." Food. Damn, I haven't eaten in a while...wonder if there's anything cheap around—

"Oh and how could I forget?" she continues. "Church is tomorrow at 10:30! It's a short walk so we can all go together."

"Er...okay." I can't remember if I was religious before I woke up in that field, but given the amount the word "Heretic" is thrown around here, I probably should be.

"Your room is upstairs," she says, handing me a key. "I'll show you where it is."

●

Claire's bobbed hair bounces slightly as she buzzes up the steps.

She's got a surprising amount of energy for an old lady. Soon we're in a long wallpapered hallway filled with small paintings of cats, flowers and landscapes. Claire pushes open the first door on the right.

It's small, but better than nothing. A twin bed is pushed against the opposite wall below a couple of windows. There's a small closet, a desk and a chair. The room smells like window cleaner.

"Now the bathroom is just at the end of this hallway, okay, hon?" She stares at me for a second. "There's a shower in there."

I smile. That was subtle of her.

"Have a good evening, now." Claire stops at the door and turns back. "Have you eaten?"

My heart leaps. "No, I—"

"Would you like something? A sandwich, maybe?"

"Actually, I mean, if it's not too much trouble, then that would be great. I haven't eaten anything since—"

"Okay, I'll be right back, Seven." Just like her brother, Claire is so friendly it's isolating.

"Actually, I might take that shower first."

Claire looks somehow relieved. "Not a problem! I'll just leave the sandwich in your room for you. Hope you like ham." She turns to leave, but once again pauses and swivels back. "Oh, by the by," she says, "I noticed you didn't have any baggage with you...and your clothes are in awful shape..."

"Oh, yeah, I...uh—"

"You don't have to tell me what happened—I've made the mistake of asking that once before." She grimaces and shakes her head. "In any case, there's a place nearby that has cheap donated clothing for sale—money goes to the blind. Just make a left from the front entrance and walk a couple of blocks—you can't miss it."

"Cool—"

"I'll get some of Adrian's clothes for you to wear in the meantime."

"Oh, I don't want to have to take his—"

"He won't mind. Adrian's a good boy."

I haven't met Adrian, but I feel embarrassed for him all the same. Oh well. There's no use fighting Claire; she's just being generous. "Well, all right then," I say. "Thanks again."

"You're welcome!" Claire moves for the door again, and this time she makes it all the way through.

•

I got a few twinges of memory on the way here. Small things. Something about the city air felt familiar, and that great missile of a Capitol Tower—it... it just stirred something up inside of me. Maybe I did live here before I woke up in that forest. I might have an apartment, a job, a bank account waiting for me somewhere in this city. But if I can't even remember my name, how am I supposed to find out anything about myself? The only thing I can do is wait it out here. If my memory doesn't come back on its own, maybe I'll run into someone who knows me and can set me straight.

The soap and hot water stings my scratches but washes away most of the stress. I am so fucking lucky. Only a day ago I was unconscious, surrounded by wildlife in some fucking forest. Now I'm refreshing myself in a shower with the amazingly beautiful knowledge that I have a warm bed and ham sandwich waiting for me.

Hopefully, I can get a job at that bookstore Claire mentioned. Who is this Adrian kid, anyway, and why does he live with his grandma? I mean, what kind of rock band is he in, anyway?

•

There's clothes on my bed—some old jeans, boxers, socks and a white T-shirt—but no food. My stomach rumbles as I dress. Then there's a knock at the door. "Come in," I say.

"Here it is!" Claire's got a sandwich and some chips. She holds out the paper plate like it just earned her first place at a state fair. "There's a glass on your bedside table; the tap water isn't too bad here."

I glance at the table and notice an old radio alarm clock—it reads 7:08 p.m. in digital red numerals. "This is amazing," I say, barely able to contain the drool. "I really appreciate it."

"Well aren't you a little gentleman!" she beams. "You're once again welcome, but I am sorry I took so long. I got distracted by that handsome President of ours. He just announced new plans to keep the Heretics down."

"Excuse me?"

"Yes, sounds like we'll soon be cleaner than a teacup!" she laughs. "Have a nice evening, dear!"

•

"Come in the water," the blond girl says, splashing some of the chemically treated liquid in my direction.
Laughter. I throw myself into it.

The leaves are everywhere—brown, yellow and red. I see her soft black jacket disappear behind the tree. I run for it and trap her against the oak.

"You were supposed to count," she whispers.

Her hair is soft in my hand—softer than it looked. "I love you," I say.

Her fingernail runs down my chest and I shiver.

•

Gentle strumming of an acoustic guitar—my eyes open. I roll over and squint at the clock—it bleeds *1:03 a.m.* The ceiling fan spins in time with the music. "That's nice," I hear myself mumble.

4
THE CHURCH

"Good morning, Seven," Claire smiles as I enter the dining room. She motions to a pair of teenagers. "Seven—Walt and Emily. Walt and Emily—Seven."

"Hi," I say.

Walt, a spiky-haired, mousy boy, cranes his neck 90 degrees and stares vacantly. Emily, a blonde with powder-white skin and small, black-rimmed glasses shoots me a quick wave. She doesn't look up from her fried egg.

The two kids probably aren't friends. Emily and Walt are so far away from each other, they're practically sitting at different tables.

A still-folded newspaper rests peacefully between the pair. The headline reads: *President Reveals New Anti-Heresy Measures*.

I grab a seat near the paper and reach for it, but my hands are intercepted by a steaming plate of eggs and toast.

"Enjoy!" sings Claire.

My left hand snaps up the toast; the right snags the newspaper. Emily gives me a weird look, but I shrug it off.

> Navy blue and gold billowed behind President William T. Drake in a televised speech yesterday at the Capitol Tower.
>
> "Heresy is at its end," he proclaimed.
>
> The President said the government is ramping up internal security to prevent what he called a "frightening spread of Heresy."

The first item under way involves updating laws and surveillance technologies, he said. "We cannot fight Heresy with outdated provisions."

Drake also announced the creation of the Department of Purity, a government branch dedicated to national unity and safety.

"We will not wait around for another Great War," Our Leader said. "The Department of Purity will ensure Heretics are dealt with efficiently. We will cut the problem out of society."

President Drake gave no further details of the plan, citing a likely danger to national security. However, he assured TV viewers that Heretics will feel the new measure's effects.

"Remember, oh great nation," said the President, "Our unity will conquer all evil."

The Church applauded the initiative.

"It's time we teach the Heretics a lesson," the Headmaster said in a statement. "There are some who don't realize the consequences of deviance. The President's plan will make them clear."

Citizens have also voiced support for the plan.

"Every time I turn on the tube there's something else those ... Heretics [have] done to try and frighten good citizens," said Bill White, a Capital resident for 20 years. "Let's get them for good."

President Drake said the plan is already "going swimmingly." More traitors are being arrested than ever before, he said.

"Purity is no longer just a dream," Drake said. "It is becoming our reality."

The President—

"Good morning, Adrian," Claire interrupts. Emily's head snaps toward the entrance.

Adrian is an obvious punk rocker, somehow managing to look confident and tortured at the same time. Long, wavy-black hair falls over dark, inset eyes. His blue jeans are worn with age and his black T-shirt looks at least a couple sizes too small.

Claire points over at me. "This is Seven, our new guest."

"Hey, how's it going?" Adrian smiles.

"All right...could be worse."

Claire hesitates. "Where did you say you were from, again, Seven?"

"From a small town up north."

"Oh, George has some friends up in Loganville! Nice place, Loganville."

"You get here last night?" Adrian asks, sitting across from me. Claire slides a steaming plate under his chin.

"Yeah, I found out about this place on the train in. Caught a taxi over."

"You should have taken the Metro. How much did that set you back?"

"Twenty, but it was entertaining at least... The driver asked me if my hands were wet."

Adrian swallows his food hard and breaks out laughing. "—He said what?"

"I don't know. Before I could ask he starts telling me about driving at 6 a.m. with some guy and his soggy daughter." I start laughing, too.

Emily stares wide-eyed at us. "You shouldn't make fun of foreigners!"

Awkward.

"You in the room first door on the right?" Adrian asks me a bit tensely.

"Yeah, why?"

"I'm next door. Hope I didn't keep you up last night with my guitar. Sometimes I just have to relax, and um, that's the best way I know how."

"Oh, yeah, no, don't worry—that's totally cool. Didn't bother me at all."

"Good," he nods, "Just knock on the wall if I'm a problem."

"I love your music," Emily interjects with a smile that visibly unnerves Adrian. Who is this girl, the queen of awkward silence?

Adrian gives me a look as if to say, "This girl has issues." He turns to Emily and says, "Thanks."

"So you play in a band?" I ask.

Adrian looks relieved. "Yeah, there's three of us—call ourselves Beacon...kind of a punk, indie thing. I sing and play guitar, and then we have a bassist and drummer."

Emily is still staring at him.

"You write the songs?" I continue.

"Yeah, well mostly. Ron and Jake know better about what they can do with their instruments, so they pretty much write their own parts into the guitar stuff I come up with." Adrian sticks a forkful of eggs into his mouth, chews and gulps. "And then Ron actually has a few really tight songs of his own where he does lead vocals."

"I like your songs better," Emily says. "Your lyrics are much more thoughtful than Ron's and—"

"Thanks," Adrian cuts her off without making eye contact. "But yeah, it's pretty cool. We actually have a concert coming up in a couple nights over at the Red Lion. If you wanna come out, I can get you in free."

My hazy recollection of Adrian's guitar playing late last night is favorable, so I say "Yeah, that would be fun." At the very least it will pass the time. Maybe they'll let me trade in my hearing for a little memory.

"Cool." Adrian goes back to his eating. I shovel down the rest of my eggs.

"Oh," I say, remembering, "Claire was saying you might be able to help me get a job around here. I'm...uh, I'm really broke."

"I know the feeling," he says, considering. "Yeah, there might be an opening at the bookstore I work at. Come with me tomorrow morning and I'll see what I can do."

"That would be awesome—"

"Don't mention it."

Claire appears. "I hope y'all are almost ready to head to church. I...I don't want to be late."

It's weird. She sounds almost afraid.

"Where's Walt?" she says in a tense whisper.

Holy shit, the kid's gone. Didn't even see him get up to leave. Emily unlocks her gaze on Claire's grandson and answers, "Walt's kind of weird."

Adrian looks down at the table like he's trying to stop himself from laughing. "Now that's ironic."

"What?" says Emily vacantly.

"Well I don't want to be late," Claire repeats. "Did you see where he went?"

Emily shrugs. "I think he went outside."

Claire shuffles toward the entrance and pulls open the front door. "Walt? You out here? Walt?" The orange tabby shoots through her legs. "No, Puss! Darn cat!"

"Is he out there?" Adrian asks.

"No, maybe he headed over without us." Claire bites her lip. "I hope, anyway. I don't want any trouble."

Trouble?

"We better just go right now," she says. "Hopefully Puss won't try to follow us."

Emily excuses herself to use the bathroom. Adrian and I abandon our dishes and follow Claire out the door.

"Are we late?" I ask Adrian.

"Nah, we still have ten minutes and the church is right around the corner," he says. "But it's good to get there a little early."

Claire paces back and forth outside the house, alternately calling for Walt, the cat, Walt, the cat. Finally, Emily joins us.

"I guess they're not coming," Claire sighs. She locks the house up and power-walks into the lead.

●

The church really is right around the corner—I'm surprised I hadn't noticed it in the taxi. The thing is massive, all steel and red tinted glass with pointed edges and a triangular steeple. The church takes up almost an entire city block, and that doesn't even include the huge lawn of marble sculptures in front.

Claire still looks uneasy. There's a line—everyone has to go through some kind of security check. Adrian looks down at his feet and kicks the grass. Emily is completely spaced out—more than before. What exactly was she was doing in the bathroom?

"Last name?" commands the Guard.

"Oh, uh—" I'm squirming like a fish on a hook.

"He's visiting," Claire explains simply. The Guard looks me over, contemplates the clouds for a few seconds, and then lets me pass.

I get a whiff of strong incense as we stride through the building's massive steel doors. "Unbelievable," I exhale almost instantly. Turns out the ground level is actually the fifth floor. There's stairs and an elevator that go down to four more, all the same size. The floor I'm on alone looks like it could seat maybe two thousand—and the place is packed! It's like a damn sports arena; sure there's a lot more candles and it's a lot quieter, but I mean, damn, there's even a giant Jumbotron hanging from the ceiling to ensure everyone has a view! How could—

Adrian chuckles. "Seven, are you all right?"

I close my gaping jaw. "Oh…yeah…I'm just—"

"Overwhelmed, right? Understandable, this is your first time in the Capital. This is one of the largest cities in the world. The Church is built to support that."

We find seats on the third level. They're not all exactly next to each other, but close enough. It's like we're the last to arrive at a fucking movie premiere.

"That couple down there makes me feel kind of underdressed," I whisper to Adrian with a laugh. I point at a silk-suited man and an astonishingly made-up woman in the front row.

"Well, they have a bit more money than you do," Adrian replies. "Wait, you do know who that is, right?"

I shake my head no, and then try to explain, "Um, I mean…it's hard to tell from here."

"That's Daniel Alexander Young… You know, owner of every other building in the city?"

I squint in an effort to pretend like I'm analyzing the man closer. "Oh yeah, so it is."

The lights cut out and a baby starts wailing. There's a slight hum from above and a cylindrical shaft of sunlight courses through the building. It immediately reveals a black-robed, balding man, who for all I know could have been standing by himself in the darkness down below the whole time. Talk about drama.

"Greetings," the priest's voice booms in digital surround. His sharp green eyes flash giant on the Jumbotron. It's hard to look away. Even the babies shut up.

"Rise!" he shouts. There's an abrupt shuffling amongst the faithful.

"Let us pray as one," he suggests. Everyone starts humming a vaguely familiar song. I pretend like I'm humming too, but no sound comes out of my mouth. Hopefully no one notices.

The screen remains focused on the priest's face. As he hums, his eyes twitch back and forth, watching, analyzing. Adrian's eyes are closed, like he's in some kind of trance. Everyone is. I'm looking at my feet, but I can still feel the heat of the priest's eyes.

The humming sinks to a pitch lower than death. I shouldn't have come here. Why did I come here?

Adrian opens an eye and gives me a funny look. I'm breathing rather heavily. I try closing my eyes, send my mind on vacation to some tropical island.

"Sit!" the priest orders. Everyone collapses back into their seats.

He smiles maniacally, like he knows something I don't. Things are getting way too cult-like for my tastes. All I want to do is leave. "Praise God for work," he says. "Praise God for love. Praise God for family. Praise God for life. Amen."

"Amen!" chants everyone.

"You know, He appreciates all of you who managed to turn up this week," the priest says, his voice like thick maple syrup. "It's come to His attention that attendance this week is nearly three less than last week. And that last week's attendance was four less than the week before. My children, we would best like to avoid another Great War."

But the place is packed! The percentage drop on that has got to be less than one!

"Why must we come to church and pray every week? Because when we were born, we each signed a contract with God: a solemn promise to serve and appease our Lord Master. Why did we sign this promise? Because we love Him, our Lord, our Master, our God.

And because we are sinners, sinners who must earn our place in His Kingdom. We have been sinners since our sinner parents committed their most sinful deed nine months before we were sinfully born. We must make our sins up to God. We must prove to Him that we are worthy of being alive in His Kingdom. We must serve Him for He is our Master!"

He pauses for an eternity. I hold my breath.

"According to the word of God, there are two gates. One leads to life, but it is narrow. The other leads to destruction, and it is wide.

"Do you know what religion literally means? Binding together! The Church is the glue that holds our nation together.

"But the Church is also what separates us from the Enemy. We are the Chosen flock of this most wretched of worlds. We are the only sinners on this forsaken planet to whom God even offers a chance to escape the flames of Hell. Only a fool would shirk off this rare opportunity for redemption! Surely no one here wants to burn for all eternity on an iron stake!"

The priest smiles as if he'd just told a clever knock-knock joke. Some people in the crowd laugh nervously. The priest glowers until silence returns.

"Children, I am afraid," he rumbles. "I am afraid that if we cannot unite under the glory of God, some Awful Judgment will come upon this land, and that the Wrath of God will arise, and there will be no Remedy.

"This cannot be allowed. If you have friends currently holding a one-way ticket to this most horrible of fates, please talk to them. Tell them that you love them. Tell them that the Church loves them. Tell them that God loves them." The priest's eyes are full of passion. "Tell them that they must love Him back or be sent to the cavernous depths of Hell! Tell them that they must serve God for He is our Lord and Master!"

I'm staring at my shoes now. I just want this to be over. I just want to get out of here.

"Yesterday, the President declared war on the Heretics. The damned can no longer be pitied. By giving up or rebelling against the force that binds us all as a people, they become traitors to their very nation. By breaking from the pack, they threaten the existence of all. They weaken our proud state and they anger God above! We are his chosen few but, I ask you, for how long? If we do not love God back, he will become vengeful and we will all pay for a few sinners' crimes!"

Silence.

"In the audience today I heard murmurs, murmurs asking, 'What can I do to help the effort? I am not in the Guard; what can I do?'

"The answer is simple: fight them from home, teach the Heretics the way. And if they cannot be taught, then they will be sent straight to Hell! We are God's chosen! He made us in his image. Any deviation is an insult to God, our Father, our Lord, our Master. To take another path is to fall into damnation! And to let another man sink into Hell is to be pulled down with him."

I glance around. It might as well be an audience of corpses.

"I sense there is someone here with doubt, someone who doesn't feel he belongs," the priest declares, his eyes glaring at me through the monitor. "Someone here is heading down the Forbidden Road." The priest's mouth clamps shut and his eyes slide back and forth.

I may have been fidgeting a little, but he can't really have seen me, right? Unless there are cameras—are we being watched? But how would he...?

The priest picks up a goblet of wine, tilts his head back and dumps the liquid down his throat. The gigantic face on the screens grins widely with stained teeth. "Let us pray for that lost soul."

The priest clasps his hands together and looks up into the light.

5
UNDER THE INFLUENCE

"You looked uncomfortable," Adrian says.

I laugh and wipe the drool off my face, take another sip and realize my beer's almost half gone. This is what, my fourth? Adrian said he'd pay for my drinks as long as I paid him back eventually, which I hope will happen soon because I could really use the money and I hate to owe people money, especially for something like alcohol, since that seems like it's kind of a waste, doesn't it? Hey, where the fuck did Jake go? He was just sitting with us a minute ago. Oh wait, yeah, he went to go flirt with some brunette broad across the room. He seemed a little tipsy, but he'd probably say I'm a little shit-faced myself so I really shouldn't be the guy judging him, I guess, right? Wait, why am I asking myself questions? That's really stupid. And wait, I'm completely ignoring Adrian, aren't I?

I clear my throat. "I was feeling uncomfortable?"

"You are such a drunk," he laughs.

I nod and take another sip.

What am I supposed to say to that, anyway? I feel like I thought of a good way to reply to that question before, but I just can't remember what it was I pieced together. On a side note, I probably shouldn't have any more to drink. Downed all those pints a little too quickly I think, maybe. Okay, come on, Seven, just think of something smart to say.

I feel my mouth stretch into a stupid grin. "Shut up."

Adrian laughs, "Don't worry, man. Not gonna accuse you of

Heresy or anything like that." He contorts his face and monotones, "We love you...God loves you... Beg for forgiveness... Rah!"

I'm pounding the table in laughter. Some proper-looking woman, sitting at the next table over, scowls at us. She really shouldn't be at a bar this late, should she? "Someone should tell that lady to go home," I try to whisper.

Adrian, apparently unbothered, continues his thought. "What they tell us at church, well, it's—"

"Brainwashing?" I finish for him.

"What? No I was just going to say it's tiring."

"Oh." I am a fucking drunk asshole, aren't I? Now he really fucking is going to call the authorities, you stupid fucking drunk asshole.

"What do you mean 'brainwashing'?" he prods. "It's church. You don't get brainwashed at church."

You stupid fucking asshole drunk, Seven. You stupid...fucking...asshole...drunk.

I sit up a little straighter in an effort to concentrate. "I'm sorry...it's just I felt like they were—I mean, everyone was so silent in the crowd. Why, um...why do you think that was?"

"Um, well...you're not supposed to talk."

"Why?"

"You're just not supposed to."

"Are you scared?"

Adrian pauses a few seconds, narrowing his eyes. His mouth opens to protest.

"—Adrian, Seven!" Jake yelps, stumbling over the table. The drummer's pole-like arms stab into the wood in a strenuous effort to right himself. Breathless and grinning, he goes on, "That girl over there, man! We were talking about our last show and she's all like, 'Do any hot guys go to your shows?' So I say 'Well, I go to my shows,' and—"

"Is that her leaving?" says Adrian, pointing.

Jake whirls around. "Shit! Wait!" He plods and careens toward the door, half-filled pint in hand.

Adrian's eyes roll. Then they regain their previous expression of outrage. "I don't get it, Seven. Is the church different where you come from?"

"Uh…well…" I sputter.

"I mean, you are a citizen, right?"

Tell him. It's okay. Just tell him.

No, I shouldn't. Fuck. "Here's the thing." And it's already coming out. Great, Seven, real great. Well you better finish what you started now, you fuck; hope they serve booze with your last supper. "I've not been completely honest. It's just I don't remember…"

Adrian's laughter makes me wince. "You don't remember?"

"I woke up two days ago…in the middle of a…well, in the middle of a forest. I don't know how I got there."

"You remember nothing before that?"

I look down at the table. "No."

"Shit, man. How much did you have to drink?"

"Tonight? Maybe four—"

"No, I mean before you woke up in a forest."

"Oh, right. I mean…" Dammit. "Heh, I wasn't drunking…er…drinking…it's like, what's it called, amm…amnesia? My mind's functioning and all, but I mean, no long-term memories. No identity."

"Are you sure your mind's functioning?"

"I think so."

"So," Adrian begins, considering. "You don't remember going to church before today?"

"Well, some of it I guess, kind of…but…"

"But you didn't feel like you belonged?"

I point at Adrian a few times before finally vocalizing "Right!"

He nods slowly. "Seven, I think we should go for a drive."

"You do?"

"Yes."

"When?"

"Right now."

•

I'm outside before I realize I've stood up.

"Where we going?" I ask as the pub's door slams noisily behind me.

"Ah, just to some empty lot near the home. It's a playground or something."

"Right." I search for a good alleyway to run down. "Did you tell me that already?"

"No."

"Did I ask why we're going there?"

"To talk," Adrian says. "Don't worry, I'm not going to kill you."

"Heh," I choke on the laugh. "Thanks."

I bend my knees to fit into Adrian's rusted silver sports car. Methodically, Adrian slips the key into the ignition and turns it. Heavy bass punches me in the gut. In a quick, apologetic motion, he shuts off the radio.

As I stare out the window, the restaurants and bars become a stream of neon. The more we drive, the worse the scenery gets. Then Adrian decides to pull into something resembling a parking lot, except I can't seem to find any painted lines. He shifts into park while I scan for prostitutes.

Why did he bring me here? "Why are we here, again?"

Adrian takes a deep breath, pauses for a second, and his voice takes on a haunting timbre. "I thought he was insane."

What the hell is he on? "You know, I'm kind of starting to think you're—"

"My dad once told me that the government's been manipulating us since the day we were born."

Oddly, this statement calms me. Maybe I won't get raped tonight.

"He said the problem is we don't recognize half the shit they've done to us. We accept the absurd, things we shouldn't be accepting. He said they've programmed us to tolerate injustice. And Seven, maybe you're proof of that. It's like you've been freed."

I think hard about this last point. George hadn't flinched when we witnessed the execution outside my train window. And I was the only one fidgeting in church.

"Okay," I say, still considering. "So I've been deprogrammed. I can tell you or anyone who cares to know that this is a fucked up country with some serious reality issues. Check. Please tell me what that does for me or anyone."

"Well, I mean, I can't speak for anyone else, but it helps me come to terms with a few things." Adrian reaches into the backseat, procures a bottle that's labeled water but smells like rubbing alcohol. "I'm being watched by the government."

"What?"

"They have this list of people they think could potentially pose a risk to their security. They're worried I might try to compromise national security." He takes a sip.

"Why? Were you arrested for something?" Wow, Seven, you certainly have a way with words tonight.

"No, it's precautionary. The Guard just believes I'm potentially dangerous to national security."

I glance at my feet.

"It's okay," he takes a gulp of the booze. "Sometimes you lose."

I frown. "Wait, it's not because of your music, is it?"

"Well," he laughs, "that doesn't help, but it's more complicated than that." He opens his palm. "My dad being executed for treason, mainly."

I'm not exactly sure what to say to this, and Adrian can't seem to bring himself to speak either. The only one with anything to add, really, is a screaming car a few blocks away.

Adrian takes another swig from his bottle. "One night when I was ten, my mom and dad went out to a dance club. It was their twelfth anniversary. In between songs, a soldier walked up to them—he wanted to dance with my mother.

"Well, my dad wanted to protest, but this was the Guard he was dealing with. He didn't want trouble, you know? Especially on their anniversary! So he relented and let it happen—I think he figured he could bear it if it was just one song."

Adrian looks down at the steering wheel. Now he looks out his window and moves his hand up to cover his eyes.

I turn my head away and look out at a swing set.

"I'm sorry, Seven, I haven't told this story for a long time."

"Hey, it's all right. You don't have to...I mean, you barely even know me, and—"

Adrian cuts me off with a look; he lets me see the infuriated tears, the fire in his eyes. "No, I really do. Talking is really helping me see how fucked up this country is; how they break you into obedience, like some fucking dog! They had me believing my dad was a lunatic, Seven! They had me believing that I needed to be watched!" He gulps down more of the liquid.

"Dad couldn't—my dad couldn't take watching the soldier dance with mom, so he excused himself to the bathroom. But when he came out a few minutes later, they were gone.

"He searched frantically around the club. He ran outside, yelling her name. He circled the block, calling her again and again. Then he heard this muffled scream.

Dad found her—and the soldier—in an alley. The demon had my mom pinned against the wall. He was—he was ripping her dress open."

"God," I manage.

"Dad took the soldier by surprise. He grabbed a brick from the ground and slammed it into the soldier's skull. The fucker got loose, yelled for help, and staggered away down the alley. But he wasn't fast enough. Dad tackled him, drove the brick into his head over and over.

"Dad told me he couldn't control himself, that the rage ignited him."

"He loved her."

"Yeah, he did," he smiles slightly. "But the judge would later call it 'the devil's influence.' After the beating, two men rushed Dad, tore him away from the red mess, slammed him against the wall. They pulled his arms hard behind his back—broke them—and snapped on the shackles.

"Dad waited a month in jail for his trial, on a diet of brown bread and water. He looked so sick when he walked into the courtroom. The prosecution said it was God's punishment for his sins. Dad tried to defend himself but he had no chance. The judge—

the honorable James T. Farnsworth—sentenced him to death for murder, Heresy and treason."

"Treason? But he was just defending his—"

"Judge Farnsworth said that killing a soldier was an attempt to undermine the unity of the nation. And in a circumstance like that, there's no self-defense or family protection claim. In this country, it's always government over family. Always. So they dropped Dad the next day."

"Dropped?"

"You know, with a rope," he slams his hand against the wheel. "Oh, and it gets worse. They televise that shit live so the whole country can watch. Mom and I didn't have to be watching to know when Dad got dropped. You could tell by the cheering next door."

"What happened to your mom?"

Adrian gazes out his window again. "She developed an addiction to painkillers. I came home from school one day and found her convulsing on the ground."

"God...I'm sorry."

Adrian smiles weakly.

"I skipped school a lot after that. I'd just sit and play guitar all day. Nights, I'd ride the Monorail around the city and listen to music. Barely anyone would be riding so I'd find the emptiest car, sit by the window and watch the lights flicker by."

I smile slightly. "Are you afraid they'll arrest you?"

"I was afraid at first," he says. "But a little while ago I decided that there's no point in being scared. When you're on the Watched List, arrest is pretty much inevitable. Sure, there's ways I could try and protect myself...quit the band, go back to school, get a 9 to 5. But then I would hate myself."

"And they still might find something on you."

"Exactly," he says. "You can't let fear run your life. I don't want to die afraid. If I have to die, I want it to happen when I'm happy. I want it to happen when I'm doing something I love."

"I saw...an execution...on my way into the city."

He eyes me.

"George...George called them rebels," I say. "Do you...I mean, have you heard anything...about...anything like that?"

Adrian slouches into his seat a bit more, stares out at the empty playground. "No."

"Oh," I say. "Okay."

"Now I have a question for you," he says.

I brace for the worst.

"Since you don't know who you are, how in Hell did you come up with the name Seven?"

"I, uh, saw the number carved on a tree."

Adrian snickers, "What?"

"Hey, it was the first thing I could think of when your uncle or whatever asked who I was!" It's strange, but I find myself chuckling again, too. Kind of embarrassing after talking about such heavy matters, so I turn to my window in an attempt to hide it. My eyes meet those of a Guard.

"Shit," whispers Adrian. "Roll down your window."

"You boys are out awful late," the intruder hisses through the sliding glass. His breath smells of garlic. "Is everything...all right?"

"Everything's fine, sir. We were just talking," Adrian answers.

"What do you...have there, son?" He points at Adrian's bottle.

"Just some water," Adrian smiles.

"Just some water," the soldier repeats, laughing slowly. "You boys better head home. This is no place to drink...water and...talk."

"Yes, sir. Thank you for your concern, sir."

The Guard grins for an instant and then backs slowly away. Adrian starts the engine. The Guard's glowing white eyes track us until we're out of sight.

"Fuck. Fuck. I did not need that," Adrian stammers.

"You think he heard us talking?"

"No, he wouldn't have let us drive off. God, they're fucking everywhere!"

●

My eyes open and we're home. I stumble out of the car, slam the door shut and follow Adrian inside. I finally make it to my room and collapse into bed. I hear the strumming of his guitar.

Fuck, I think I'm still drunk. Or maybe I'm just tired? Or

maybe there's just too much on my mind. I just need some sleep; I'll be able to think tomorrow. Dammit, where did that guy come from?

A knocking at my door jolts me out of my daze and for an instant I think it's the Guard again.

"You still up, man?" I hear. The guitar music has stopped.

"Uh, yeah," I lie, getting out of bed and turning the light on in a quick motion. I open the door and Adrian enters.

"I...wasn't completely honest with you, Seven," he says. He's holding something—a card. He pushes it into my hands. White creases and a small matte image of a black figure with fiery red eyes break through its glossy surface. The image is familiar—it's the same as I saw in the Monorail station. "I do know something about rebels."

"Where did you get this?"

He laughs. "This one gig I did, man. Backstage after the show I met this brunette, Ana. We get to talking and before I know it we're back at my room—"

"Where is this going?"

He cackles. "All right. To make things short, I wake up the next morning—the girl is gone and the card is on my desk. Take a look at the back."

I flip it over and read, scrawled in white, *Adrian—Thanks for an exceptional show. Call me if you're ever in trouble. xoxo Ana.* And below, a phone number.

"I never heard from her again!" he says, suddenly grinning. "Nice, right? I got used!"

I take a step back. "So did you call her?"

"Dude, don't you understand what happened? This is basically an invite to the Underground!"

"How do you know?"

"Did you see Fire-Eyes on the front? It's the Underground!"

"But, wait, why would they hand out their phone numbers on business cards? Wouldn't that leak pretty damn easy?"

"Fuck if I know, dude. I'm sure they're all high tech and shit. Anyway, this girl liked me."

What the hell does that mean? Still, the fact I've seen the

symbol does add to the card's credibility. The phone number is all 2s, 3s, 4s and 7s, so I memorize it, just in case he's right.

"I've been kind of wanting to call, but...well I know I'm being watched...I don't want to jeopardize what these guys are doing..."

"Nah man," I reply, "I'm sure they're all high tech and shit."

"Hey shut up!" he bursts, snatching the card back. "Well, even if I never do call, this will always be a memento."

"You sound pretty smitten with these guys."

"No, no, not that," he laughs, holding the card high over his head. "This commemorates the best sex of my life!"

I groan.

Adrian grins. "Well, with that image painted firmly in your head, I'll let you get some sleep. Have a good night!"

"Night," I smile wearily. I close the door after him and crawl back into bed.

•

Then there's another violent knocking.

"Seven, if you still want a job, get the hell up!" The muffled yell is Adrian's.

I glance at the clock. We're going to be late.

6
HISTORY

We make it to work with two minutes to spare. Somehow, I don't have a hangover.

The place is one of those mega-bookstores: two huge floors connected by tall, slow-moving escalators. Adrian quickly explains the layout: most of the books are on the main floor, while music and periodicals are on the second. I'm curious about the history section, but the priority is getting hired.

"Hmm, I'm not exactly sure where our manager is," Adrian mumbles, turning toward a curved booth labeled *Information* where a young woman with bright red hair sips on a cup of coffee.

"Yeah," I say. "The .nformation desk is probably a good place to start."

"Smartass," Adrian grins. "Hey Sarah, do you know where Bill is?"

She looks up from her paperback novel, beady-eyed like a squirrel. "Good morning, Adrian! I think I saw him head for the café!"

"Thanks," Adrian smiles, and then, pointing to me, "This is my friend, Seven. Trying to get him some work."

"Awesome! Pleasure to meet you, Seven!" she chirps.

"Second floor," Adrian says, turning toward the escalator. "Hey, by the way, that nice girl back there? Stay away, she's a freak."

"Good to know."

The aroma of coffee and baked goods hits my nostrils midway up the stairway. My stomach growls; all I've eaten today is an apple. We walk past a row of magazines. Half of them have President Drake on the cover.

"All right, that's him over there," Adrian motions toward a burly and balding man with thick, black-rimmed glasses and amazingly pale complexion. He's chewing on a donut. "Just answer him exactly like I told you and you'll have the job, easy."

I hope so. I really need this. What am I going to do if I get turned down? I won't even know where to begin.

"Bill!" Adrian calls out.

The man puts down the pastry and wipes his hands vigorously with a napkin. "Good morning, Adrian," he coughs. Bill's listless gaze shifts to me. "Friend of yours?"

"Hi," I say.

"This is Seven," Adrian says. "He's looking for a job, and I heard we had an opening."

"You heard correctly," Bill frowns. "Hello, Seven. Do you have any experience in a place like this?"

"Yes," I lie, "I used to work in a store like this on the other side of town."

"Good, good," he says, still chewing. "Why did you leave?"

"They went out of business."

"Hm…good reason. Have you been through school?"

"Yes, I graduated from National University."

Bill's eyes light up. "Ah, my alma mater! A great school!"

"Oh yeah, I loved it."

Bill nods. Adrian elbows me in the rib.

"Go Birds!" I exclaim.

"Ha! Yes, go Birds!" Bill bursts. "Well, all right Seven. Usually I'd have you fill out an application, but you seem like a good person and I trust Adrian. Is ten an hour okay?"

Score! "Yeah, awesome, that will be fine."

"Excellent!" he beams. "No one's at the music and movie information desk right now, so head over there. I'll give you some paperwork to fill out later—tax stuff."

Adrian offers me a thumbs-up.

Bill continues, "Adrian, you stay with him until he gets the hang of things."

•

Adrian leads me to a booth on the other side of the escalator. "See, I told you. Bill's such a pushover."

"Heh," I manage, turning my head to make sure my new manager didn't hear. Bill makes wings out of his greasy hands by crossing the thumbs and yells "Go Birds!" again.

"How are the ol' Birds doing, anyway?" I ask Adrian.

"Well," he says, "last time I checked, they were locked in the cellar without a key."

"Shame, that."

The information desk is made of a light pine, or at least a veneer that looks like it. There's a small, black flat-screen monitor and keyboard. Adrian and I take seats in the chairs and sink below the counter.

"All right, Seven," Adrian says. "Nothing too difficult here. People walk up and ask you about an album or movie. You smile and say 'Allow me to check' or, you know, something lame like that, and then you turn to this computer over here." Adrian grabs the mouse. "Select either title, artist or keyword in the drop-down menu, type it in here, press enter, and voila! All the information they could ever need."

"Should I say 'voila' when I find what they want?"

"No, that would probably be awkward," he says, standing. "Now, they may ask you to personally guide them in the right direction. Everything's ordered alphabetically and by genre, so it shouldn't take you too long. Plus I think the computer even displays a map." Adrian bends over the keyboard and scrolls the screen. "Yeah, right here."

"Great. So what do you do when no one needs information?"

"A lot of people just sit here and look detached. Personally, I like to do some reading."

"I didn't bring a—" I stop short and look around the store. "Oh, right."

"You're a quick one, aren't you?" Adrian laughs.

"Shut up. You mind if I go get something?"

"Go ahead, but make it quick. Bill's almost done his breakfast of champions."

•

I run down the escalator, scanning the first floor as I descend. I'm looking, of course, for the history section—I've gotten curious about that damn war everyone keeps talking about, the war that turned a forest into a cemetery.

My eyes catch a sign that says *History*, and I sprint over. Got to make this quick. I run a finger against the book spines until I come across one called *War Against Heresy*. I pop it out and dash back to the escalator. The girl at the information desk—I forget her name already—sends me a look of bewilderment.

"Are you one of us?" she calls, her head slowly craning to follow my ascent.

"Looks like it."

She sticks her thumb up in the air and shouts, "Sweet!"

•

I fall back into my chair with a sigh. Adrian tilts his head and squints at my book. "Want to learn about the Great War, huh?"

"I just want to find out what was so damn great about it."

Adrian laughs, and then whispers back, "Maybe we can talk about it later."

I turn to an introductory section of the book, titled *The Greatest of All Wars*, and nearly throw up right there on the page. I mean, hey, what if people deem a new war even greater? What then?

> In a war against such atrocious Heresy, one must be astonished that it actually lasted as long as it did. Even with God on the Republic's side, the Heretics had in them a ferocious energy that only the Devil himself could keep burning inside their black, demonic hearts. The War Against Heresy quickly turned into the bloodiest war in our history. Heavy losses were dealt to both sides, but after four long years the Republic finally came out victorious!
>
> It all began five years previously when Joseph Fink, Devil Incarnate, began a new church in the Capital!

"This thing reads like an adventure novel," I mutter.

Adrian looks over. "You think it's biased?"

"A little," I smirk.

"Huh," remarks Adrian, considering, "Yeah, I read that book in school. Never felt like I was getting the whole story. I asked George about it once. He told me the book was pretty accurate, of course."

Sounds about right.

> Frighteningly, Fink lured a great many people into his demonic cult. At first the government had brushed it off as a passing fad. They were unprepared for the horror that was to come.
>
> Explosives were set off in the basement of the Capitol Tower. Within minutes, the heart of our nation was reduced to rubble. Though many made it out of the building alive, including our great President Frederick Wright, many more did not. Among the dead were the Vice-President and the First Lady.
>
> It was a shockwave that ripped the nation through its very core. The perpetrators were captured within hours by a country hungry for answers. It was soon revealed that the bombers were members of Fink's clan. President Frederick Wright ordered the immediate arrest of Joseph Fink. Meanwhile, the citizens still pure of heart heard the call of God Himself and burnt down the central lair of the evil Heretics.
>
> The capture of Fink and the destruction of the misbelievers' largest hive enraged the Devil. With a wave of the Evil One's sharp claws, the Heretics ignited with a passion both tremendous and unforeseen. The great fury spread like a virus and soon everywhere there was fighting and bloodshed.
>
> Acting quickly, President Wright mobilized the famed Guard and—

"Excuse me?" compels a voice, feminine and cool. She's gorgeous. I become mesmerized in the way her golden hair curls just slightly at the shoulders. Adrian opens his mouth to speak, but I beat him to it.

"Can I help you?"

She looks about my age, I think. "Yes, I was looking for a particular album…"

Her ocean blue eyes meet mine. I shiver slightly, smile and

type whatever she says into the computer. Tragically, the message *Out of stock* appears.

"We don't seem to have it," I lament. "Rock album, huh? Who do you like?"

She smiles. "Yeah, I listen to stuff like…" She lists a bunch of bands I don't know. That's not important. The wheels are in motion.

I smile and nod until she finishes, and then say, "I was actually planning to see a concert for this local band tomorrow night…"

Adrian gives me a funny look. Then he drops his eyes, smiles and shakes his head.

I continue, "If you're not doing anything, I'd like to…"

Now *she* gives me a funny look.

"I mean…would you like to…um, meet at the show and, um…I don't know…rock out, or—?"

"That sounds like fun! I'm kind of in a hurry right now though, so, uh, call me later, okay?" She smiles, and grabs a pen and piece of paper from thin air. "My name is Kira," she declares.

"I'm Seven," I respond tremulously, eyes on the note. "You have nice handwriting."

Out of the corner of my eye, I notice Adrian burying his face in his hands.

"Thanks," Kira says, sliding the number across the counter. Then she gives me a look as if she knows something I don't. "Well… thanks for your help, Seven. I'll have to try somewhere else I suppose. Nice meeting you." She stretches her hand over the desk.

I shake it. "Yeah, you too. I'll…uh…I'll talk to you later."

"Sounds good! Bye!" she says, turning away.

I watch Kira all the way to the escalator. Her eyes float back in my direction for a brief instant. Then she descends out of sight.

7
GLORY DAYS

Adrian hands the cashier a ten.

"I promise I'll pay you back," I say.

Adrian collects the change and smiles. "I'm not worried about it. So what are your plans with that girl?"

"Dunno. I'll call her later and figure stuff out, I guess."

"Cool. Nothing expensive I hope," Adrian frowns slightly as he looks into his wallet.

"It's a first date; we'll do pizza or something."

He smiles again and hands me some more cash. "This should cover the pizza and any other random fun."

"Thanks."

A bored looking, greasy-faced teenager steps out of the kitchen and slaps a tray on the counter. Then he half-heartedly tosses our wrapped sandwiches, fries, and drinks onto its surface. "Have a good day," he yawns.

I grab the tray and we find a booth near the door. My side's red seat is torn, but it's still a relief after standing in that line for so long—ironic, considering they call this fast food. I tear at the sandwich's wrapping and throw it aside. "Glad I don't work here."

"Eh...Bill had me organizing books," Adrian says, holding a fry thoughtfully between his fingers. "That sucked."

"At least you got exercise. I was sitting at the desk the whole time. Guess how many people needed information after you left?"

Adrian shrugs as he bites into his burger.

"One—he wanted to know where the restroom was."

"You're pretty funny for a guy with no memory."

"Thanks," I say with a munch. The hamburger is mediocre, but I can't stop eating; I'm so hungry. The refreshingly cool, bubbly soda also tastes infinitely better than it probably really is. "So are you ready for your gig tomorrow night?" I ask.

"Yeah, probably. I mean, before shows I get a little nervous, but when I get out on the stage and hear that crowd... the adrenaline kicks in, you know?"

I'm mid-bite, so I nod. My eyes stray to a kid at the table next to ours. She's struggling to tear open the wrapping of a tiny, really cheap-looking blue sand shovel. Her mother eventually leans over to help. This also fails. Mom shoots up and stomps toward the pimple-ridden teen at the counter, package in hand. "Excuse me!" she seethes.

"—Anything else you need?" Adrian asks.

"Oh, uh..." My head flicks back in his direction. "Actually, you have any old watches I can borrow? Don't want to be late."

Adrian nods over my shoulder at a glass display of merchandise. "You don't want a Spy Boy watch?"

"I'm not using your money on something that's going to break."

"Yeah, right, you just don't want Kira to see you in a big, shit-plastic watch," he smirks. "Of course you can borrow one of mine. Remind me when we get back home."

"Thanks. I really owe you, man."

He waves his hand like a magician. "I think you'll have a good time at the show. Our music is pretty good for dates, I think." He cackles. "The chicks have a tendency to go wild."

"I guess you'd know."

"I would," he says. "So learn anything from that history book?"

I wince. "Maybe. I don't know. It was kind of agonizing to read, honestly. Maybe you could clear a few things up for me."

"I consistently got C's in history," he says, putting down the burger. "But I suppose you could try me."

"Well, for one thing, I don't understand why the war started."

"Oh, that's easy," Adrian says. "Joseph Fink equals one...evil...dude. Oh, and he blew up the Capitol Tower."

"But, why did he do that? Wasn't he just head of a rival church?"

"Yeah, an *evil* church."

"But..."

"I don't know, man, I think maybe I'm not the best person to ask about this. Maybe there's a better book in there."

"Yeah." I look down at my plate and my food is gone. "Well, that was pretty good."

"You say that now," Adrian says, licking his fingers. "Talk to me in an hour."

•

I step off the escalator and find an old man in an obnoxious lime-green polo and checkered pants leaning against my booth.

I clear my throat. "Excuse me, sir, can I help you?"

George spins around. "Why, hello Seven!" he exclaims. "Claire told me you got a job here with Adrian, so I thought I'd stop by and see how things were working out at the hostel!"

"Oh, uh, yeah, everything is fine," I stutter. "Um, how are you?"

"I'm just grand. Just came from a game of—" He swings an invisible club, holding the follow-through long enough to watch the invisible ball sail into the magazines. "Do you play?"

"Not really, no."

"Shame! Great sport!"

I walk behind the desk and notice my copy of *War Against Heresy*. "George, you said you were a soldier in the Great War, right?"

"I was a lieutenant!" he beams.

"I was thinking recently that I...that I really don't know a lot about the war besides what they taught in school," I say. "Could I ask you a few questions? I mean, since you were there when it all happened."

"Why of course! I'd be delighted!" George pops. Then he leans in close and whispers, "Aren't you on shift?"

"Eh, all I've done so far is sit here, and they probably won't get mad at me for talking to a veteran," I say with a motion toward the empty seat. "Why don't you join me until Adrian gets back?"

"Grand idea!" George yells, ratcheting himself into the chair. "So what would you like to talk about?"

I ponder this question for a bit. Where to start? "Well, I've been a bit confused about how it began. Did the government just...were they just reacting to the growing influence of, um, Joseph Fink?"

George laughs inexplicably. "Oh my, no! Is that what they teach nowadays?"

I shrug. "I mean—"

"Fink's religion...well, it was more than a religion you see. Fink was creating an army. But it was a different kind of army than the Guard—who weren't called that back then—they were just the Army in those days—I believe they were renamed sometime after the war ended." George grins broadly at this vague recollection. "Fink's army was never really big enough or experienced enough. So they used fear tactics." George swallows.

"Fear tactics?"

"Yes, fear tactics," he pauses again, this time to smack his lips. "Seven, do you think I might be able to get a drink?"

"Yeah, there's a café over there and a water fountain in the other direction," I say, motioning with my hands.

"Thank you, my boy. We'll pick this story up in a minute." George heads for the fountain.

"Hey," a teenager greets. "Where's the, like, restroom?"

"In the back," I say. "But you need a token." I hand him one, tiny and gold.

"Token? That's pretty bullshit."

"Store policy," I try to explain, but he's already on his way.

George returns with a wet spot on his shirt. "Where were we?"

"Fear tactics."

"Ah yes, fear tactics. That's what Fink's army used," George pauses to look vacantly at a twenty-something girl in a mini-skirt getting off the escalator. He calls out, "Miss, do you need any help?"

She turns her head awkwardly in George's direction. "No, I'm good…thanks."

"You're most welcome!"

"They'll come to us if they need help," I tell him.

"That's not the service attitude we had in my day," he replies grimly.

I shrug.

"So what was I talking about?"

"Fear tactics."

"Ah yes, fear tactics. That's what Fink's army used. Well, no, I suppose the proper term would be guerilla tactics. Are you familiar with guerilla tactics?"

"Yeah, I think so."

George explains anyway. "Guerilla tactics are untraditional and some would say unfair maneuvers by an army to gain an advantage. Fink's army would target soldiers and members of the government individually—when they weren't prepared. There were a lot of assassinations. Then it escalated.

"Fink started employing explosives in his attacks, and he began using them against anyone who didn't belong to his new order," he says, taking a long, wheezy breath. "And then the bastards blew up the Capitol Tower. The first lady and…some other government official, I think, was killed." George frowns and shakes his head. "So, President Wright—he was president at the time—President Frederick Wright—well, he was left with no option but to launch a full-scale attack on Fink's soldiers."

"Wait, I read that he just ordered Fink's assassination… and then the citizens blew up his…his evil lair or something."

George considers this. "Oh yes, you're right, you're right. Well, mostly, anyway. Is that what they're teaching these days?"

I shrug. "I mean—"

"Wright ordered Fink's arrest, as you said. But the Patriots acted on their own. You have to remember Fink's religion was accepted at first…before all the fear tactics. That came later. His chapels were all over the place at one time. Did you see the one at the cemetery when you were visiting?"

"That was...?"

"You betcha. Abandoned now, of course—awful place. Anyway, Patriots burnt down all of Fink's chapels...including the biggest one of all...the one where Fink and his army were based.

"We thought it was over after that, but we were sorely mistaken. Suddenly all the Heretics came out of the woodwork. There were more explosions, more deaths, only now most citizens were fighting back. There were men, women, children—there really were few who did not fight in one way or another.

"Now, I was with the army, so I was involved in much more focused combat—the kind of fighting that really won the Great War."

"Right."

"You know, I once fought near that cemetery you visited. The government had just discovered that—"

"Yeah, I think you told me about that on the train."

"Oh, yes, I did, didn't I? How silly of me. It was just such a breathtaking battle." He wipes a tear from his eye. "Poor old Jimmy didn't make it, sadly. After he went down...shot between the eyes...I dedicated every kill to that brave soul.

"You know I visited his family after the war. Told 'em the story, how I dedicated every kill to that brave soul. Know what they said?"

"Wha—"

"They said 'God bless you, son. God bless you.'"

"Excuse me," a voice interrupts. The girl who George previously accosted is standing over us.

"Yes, dear?" George answers, scrambling to his feet.

"I'm looking for an album."

"Photos?" George shoots back excitedly.

"No?" she says, eyes narrowing. "Music."

I push George gently back into his chair and take over. "Who's the artist?"

"Corey Jacobs."

Four titles pop up. Two are out of stock. "And which album are you looking for?"

"Shirtless."

It's out of stock—figures—good thing I'm not paid on commission. "Sorry, don't seem to have that one. We can order—"

"No!" She spins away with a harrumph.

I turn back to George. "So he was caught, right?" I continue.

"Who?"

"Fink."

"Is that what they're teaching these days?"

Pause. "Yeah."

"Well, yes, he was. But then he got away again—maybe they don't talk about that anymore. It didn't matter though—his escape I mean. The war was over and...well, we tortured him a great deal." George laughs at this. "If he's still out there somewhere, he's a fly with no wings!"

I wince at the image. "So you don't think he's at all involved with the Heretics around today?"

"Not a chance. If there's any one figure behind the current outcrop, it would have to be someone with financial influence. That's not Fink. Anyway, I'm not too worried about the Heretic situation. After the Great War, Wright—he was president at the time—President Frederick Wright—instituted a lot of new laws and security measures to make sure it wouldn't happen again."

I can't help but think Adrian's parents were victim to those measures. George must not have had much love for Claire's children. "Adrian told me about his father," I try.

George shifts in his seat and casts me a vicious look. "I don't want to talk about that."

"Hey, Uncle George," a voice interrupts.

"Adrian, my boy!" George ensnares him with a hug and vigorously shakes his hand. "How are you?"

"Can't complain," Adrian smiles. "What brings you here?"

"Oh, I just wanted to check in on our new friend Seven here...and I wanted to invite the both of you out to lunch."

"Oh, uh, we just ate," Adrian says awkwardly.

George chortles through the discomfort. "I was referring to tomorrow, of course!"

"Oh," he hesitates. "Yeah, I guess tomorrow would be okay. Fine with you, Seven?"

"Yeah, sure." Like I have any plans. Besides, maybe George will pay for the meal.

8
MINDLESS

My head keeps running over and over what happened with that girl Kira. Something about it just doesn't seem right—maybe it's the timing. She's too beautiful not to pursue, though. The best thing to do for now, probably, is distract myself—at least until it gets late enough to call her. Right now it's time for a little television.

A mustachioed man greets me and proceeds to sell a cooking device that sucks the juice out of fresh meat.

Click. The channel changes to a heavily made-up woman lamenting, "Oh Jonathan, how could you have done it?"

"It's just a cell phone," he quips.

"Just a cell phone?!" she screams. "Don't you have any understanding of what it means to her?! Don't you have any comprehension of what she means to me?! I hate you! I hate you!" Angry tears fill her eyes. She reaches into a drawer, pulls out a pistol.

Click.

"You're watching DAY-TV. 'Angry Rednecks' will be back after a few messages."

Click.

A young man with a huge smile and spiky hair declares, "Coming up, a woman who used the money she won from the lottery to launch her singing career! You'll never guess who it is!"

Click.

"But, but... how the hell we gonna destroy the heroes?" an ugly man asks a scarred pirate-looking fellow in a black-and-white striped prison-bird outfit.

"Easy, Captain Bad," the buccaneer seethes. "All we have to do is to make them fight amongst themselves. Then when they're at their weakest, we strike. Ha ha ha ha ha ha ha ha ha ha ha ha ha—"

Click.

A poorly animated boy with an almost cringingly cute voice complains to no one in particular out the window of his room: "I have a test tomorrow and I still don't understand what patriotism is! If only somebody could help me!"

"Hey Billy," a creepy, upbeat voice answers. "I think I know somebody who can,"

"Really, Mr. Narrator? Who?"

Wow. This looks so awful it just might have potential.

"No, Billy," booms another, deeper voice triumphantly. "'Who' is what owls say!" A large golden hawk flies in through the window.

Billy's jaw drops like he's having a massive orgasm. "Oh gosh! It's the National Hawk!"

"Yes, and don't call me Natty!"

Billy laughs giddily. "I won't, Mr. Hawk. I won't!"

"So I hear you want to learn about patriotism. Well son, I'm just the bird to help!"

"Hooray!"

The National Hawk turns to the camera with a huge grin that's somehow toothy. "Patriotism is something you do every day! It's the simple act of supporting your country through thick and thin! It's about smiling and never questioning your elders!"

"What is there to question, Mr. Hawk?"

"Beats me, Billy! But it seems there are some people who don't have as much faith in our nation as you or I."

"That's horrible, Mr. Hawk. If I met someone like that, why, I don't know what I'd do."

"Nor would I," the bird says gravely. "But fear not, the famous Guard are always working to yank those weeds right out of the garden!"

Billy laughs. "Hey, Mr. Hawk, can I use that line on my big test?"

"You sure can, Billy. But before I go, I want you to meet someone." The Hawk picks Billy up in his talons.

I spot Claire out of the corner of my eye and instinctively switch the channel to a news program.

"Oh hello, Seven," she greets warmly. "Anything good on?"

"Not really."

"Television has gotten so bad lately. The only show I ever watch anymore is Funnyman Dan."

I nod vaguely.

"Such a silly young man, always getting into trouble."

"Uh huh."

"Now what was I...? Oh yes!" Claire holds up a yellow box labeled *RAT-B-GONE XTRA*.

"Rat problem?" I ask.

"Oh, nothing to worry about. Nothing this won't take care of, anyway. Claire kneels by the wall and tilts the box—a white powder pours out. "This stuff is ten times more effective than the usual poison pellets, according to that nice man on the tube."

I smile at her.

Claire leaves, so I flick back to the cartoon. Now Billy and the Hawk are in a very official looking office.

"Wow, Mr. Hawk. Am I where I think I am?"

"You sure are, Billy! This is the famous Presidential Office! And here's who I wanted you to meet!" The Hawk points a wing somewhere off screen. A poorly animated President Drake, grinning like a fool, enters the scene.

"Gee whiz! You're President Drake!" Billy screams like a girl at a rock concert. A camera flashes as Drake shakes Billy's hand. Then, without saying a word, the President strolls away.

"Wow, Mr. Hawk! This has been the best day of my life!"

"Mine too, Billy. Mine too."

The End flashes onto the screen. I reach for the remote to turn the putrid machine off. My fingers hit the side and it falls onto the floor. Damn it.

"We interrupt this broadcast of 'Billy's World' to bring you down into the underground recesses of the Capitol Tower, where an execution is in progress," a thick male voice booms enthusiastically. His voice speeds up to add, "Children and the faint of heart may not want to view the following."

There's a woman with a black bag over her head and a noose around her neck. She is quiet. The camera zooms out to include a pretty blonde in a powder blue suit. She holds a microphone in one hand—it reads *DAY* in big white letters. She speaks into it: "In an insane rage, Hannah Johnson tried mailing the President an envelope packed with poisonous chemicals! Fortunately, the letter was intercepted and Johnson was caught! Now she awaits her punishment!" The prisoner starts to whimper. Seconds pass. There's a pop and she falls off camera.

"Well," says the reporter, dusting her hands. "That's the end of that."

I mute the TV, recline on the couch and look at the ceiling for a long time, transfixed. Adrian told me they televised executions, but his warning didn't make watching it any less screwed up.

I should just change the channel—get my mind off this.

Click. Another soap opera. Great.

Renewed boredom replaces the horror. Now what? I feel like I need to do something, but I can't figure out what. It's too early to call Kira about the show I think. Need to wait at least another hour or two. God, how can I be so bored? What can I do?

I must look absolutely listless; I don't feel like getting up at all. But on the other hand, that super rat poison is starting to smell ten times the smell of normal poison pellets.

●

I can tell Adrian is listening to music before I even make it up the stairs. I knock. The sound cuts out. There's some shuffling and the door swings open.

"What's up?" Adrian greets urgently.

"I'm bored out of my mind."

"Anything on TV?"

"Tried it. Watched someone get killed."

"Right," he nods. "Man, I still can't believe that girl today."

"Hm?"

"Your girl, dude!"

I exhale. "Oh, right."

Adrian laughs and waves me into the poster-plastered room. "Want to listen to some tunes?" He moves for the stereo. "This group is a little hardcore, but—"

Something on the bed's caught his attention; he stares wide-eyed and open-mouthed. "You have to be fucking kidding me!"

"What?"

Adrian's fingers pick at the fleece blanket, lift something invisible up to his eyes. "Becky!" he exclaims. "I dated her like three years ago, and I'm still finding her hair! That girl shed like a cat!"

"You're sure it's hers?"

"Positive. She's the only blonde I ever got anywhere with," he says, carefully dropping the evidence into a waste paper basket. "Becky," he whispers with a shake of his head.

I wonder if I'll get anywhere with my blonde. She was pretty cute, if I remember right. I hope I get to kiss her. Wonder if we'll—?

"Anyway," says Adrian. "Yeah. This band is really cool." He turns the volume up to a level where we can no longer really communicate. I sit on the floor, lean against the bed, face the speakers.

I close my eyes and try to picture Kira. Instead I see Hannah Johnson on the gallows. "Next up is Seven!" says the reporter in the powder blue outfit. Suddenly it's me awaiting execution. "Ready, Seven?"

"But I didn't do anything!" I protest.

"Not a problem!"

There's a pop and I start to fall.

"Well," says the reporter. "That's the end of that."

•

"Dude, wake up," says Adrian. I'm back in the room and it's quiet. "Haha, you totally fell asleep! Work wasn't that hard today, man!"

I shake my head and exhale—my mouth feels and smells disgusting.

Call her.

"Oh fuck, what time is it?"

"Like..." Adrian looks over at the clock. "Fifteen after eight."

"Shit. There's a phone in my room, right?"

"Should be. You calling?"

I nod, take a deep breath, and stagger to my feet.

"Good luck, dude."

I close the door behind me, consider my game plan, and quickly realize I have none.

This is ridiculous. I wake up in a forest with no idea of who I am. I find my way into a city I don't feel a part of, and what do I do? I ask the first cute chick I see out to a concert! I don't have time for dating—what the hell am I thinking? Anyone else in my situation would probably just focus on one thing at a time, maybe wait things out a bit before getting involved in anything. Amnesia rule number one—or at least number three—must be to refrain from getting caught up in a relationship until you work your own life out again. I mean, fuck, what if I have a girlfriend? God, what if I'm married? What if...what if I have some baby wailing for me somewhere?

But I'm lonely. Maybe she could help me figure things out. It will be easier having someone for support. And anyway, why can't I have a little fun? There's nothing wrong with this.

●

I'm still staring at the telephone. Fuck, Seven, just call her already.

I flatten out the scrap of paper I'd anxiously crumpled in my left palm and slowly dial the handwritten number into the phone.

"Idiot!" I yell—forgot to pick up the receiver. Stop being so fucking nervous!

I try the process again.

"Hello?" Kira's voice catches me off guard.

"Hey Kira, this is Seven...from the bookstore."

"Oh, hi Seven! How are you?"

"Not bad, you?"

"I'm great, thanks! Refreshing you're not one of those guys who waits three days to call a girl."

I chortle nervously. "Well, the concert is tomorrow night."

"True," she laughs.

"So, uh, yeah, about that… Doors open at ten, apparently, but I was thinking we could go eat somewhere first."

"Okay!"

"But, um, I'm actually kind of new in town. The concert's at the Red Lion, but I don't really know what restaurants or whatever are nearby."

"Oh," she says, "Well the Red Lion is actually on the boardwalk, so we could probably find a pizza place or something."

"Oh, all right." Nice, I was worried she'd demand something expensive.

"I can't wait!" she exclaims. "So how about we just meet outside the boardwalk Metro, and we'll go from there?"

"Yeah sounds good. What time do you think, like nine?"

"Okay! Hey, who's the band by the way?"

"Oh, yeah, they're called Beacon. I'm friends with the guitarist."

"Oh, I heard they're good! Wait a second… was this guitarist the guy next to you?"

I laugh like a doofus. "Yeah, actually."

"I knew I'd seen him somewhere. In fact I was going to ask, but then some other boy caught my attention."

Other boy? "Who?"

Kira laughs.

"Oh," I say, understanding. I laugh, cough, and laugh some more. "Well, all right then, I'll see you there, I guess."

"You guess correctly."

"All right, well, good night."

"Good night!" Click.

"Well that was awkward," I tell the room.

"Smooth, man." My head snaps to the door that's apparently been open. Adrian's standing there, grinning like a cat.

"You been there the whole time?"

"Since the first 'Hey,'" he says, lowering his voice in mockery. "I liked when you reminded her you were from the bookstore—she might have thought you were some other guy named Seven."

"Hey, shut up."

Adrian snickers. "Just busting your balls, man. You sounded fine."

"Good." Long pause. "So..."

"You want something to eat? I think we missed dinner but there's probably leftovers or something."

"Oh, um," I consider.

"That's actually why I was at the door, by the way. I thought the phone call would have been over already."

"I needed to prepare!" I protest, laughing. "But yeah, can we like raid the fridge or something? I'm starving!"

●

It's after midnight and I can't sleep—keep thinking about tomorrow. I hope things go okay with Kira. Of course they will. Fuck. I have work tomorrow. Why can't I fall asleep?

Violent knocking. My eyes snap open. A red *3:02 a.m.* glows through the darkness. The pounding gets louder, but it's not coming from my door.

The mumbling of an elderly woman fades into the sound of creaking stairs. Claire.

I rise from bed, walk slowly into the hallway without making a noise. Wind screams into the house. I flatten out on my stomach and creep toward the steps' edge.

Downstairs, a man ducks in from the dark. Wisps of gray streak his otherwise black hair. He wears a midnight blue trench coat and a steely glare.

"Hello," says Claire nervously.

"I need to speak with Adrian," the stranger declares.

Someone taps me on the shoulder. "Go back to bed. Everything is fine." Adrian stares at me with an expression that contradicts his reassurance. "He always shows up nights before I play."

9
BLOOD TIES

I close my menu. Thank God George is paying. On my budget, there's no way I could afford a fish place—oh wait, my mistake, it's called the Fish *Palace,* isn't it?

The waitress appears. Adrian orders the fried jumbo shrimp. I order the fried flounder.

"How's the sole?" George asks.

"It's very good."

"Is it fresh?"

"Well…"

"It's not frozen, is it?"

"Yes, but it's still very—"

"I don't want that. Is his flounder fresh?" he says, indicating me.

"Yes. Came in this morning."

"And the salmon?"

"Yes, that too."

"I'll have the salmon. Tell the chef not to overcook it."

"Okay. Do you want the full portion or the half portion?"

"Hm…how much bigger is the full?"

Adrian's eyes lower to the table. He fiddles with the white cloth napkin.

"Well, it's two times the size of the half," she says, absorbing George's look of sheer bewilderment. "The half portion isn't really enough unless you're getting a large appetizer."

"I don't want an appetizer."

"So the full portion then?"

"Yes—the full portion. Tell the chef not to overcook it."

The waitress smiles weakly. She whisks my menu away.

"You know, Seven," George initiates. "I don't believe you ever told me why you came to the Capital."

I hesitate. The waitress takes Adrian's menu.

"I had some time off," I say. "Wanted to get away, you know."

Adrian nods approvingly. George keeps staring, expecting me to continue.

"And, um," I try, "I'd never made it out to the Capital, before, so, uh, yeah."

Our server goes for George's menu.

"Fantastic!" he exclaims with a sudden clap that sends the waitress flailing back against an adjacent table. Red in the face, she again leans in, this time securing her quarry without obstacle. "I like a boy with a spirit for adventure!"

I smile weakly.

"You know, the Guard is looking for brave young men such as yourself!"

The strength of my expression fails to improve. I look over at Adrian; he's currently gazing at a blond bombshell on the other side of the restaurant.

"A lot of wonderful times I had in the military. You know I was promoted to lieutenant by the end of it!"

I'm beginning to suspect it's not just senility that makes George talk about his past so much. It was probably the happiest time of his life. Back then, he had direction and purpose. Now what is the old man doing with his life?

"So have you ever considered it?" he prods.

"Joining the Guard?"

"Indeed."

"I've thought about it," I lie. "But I wanted to sort some other things out first."

He melts. "That's admirable. Adrian, on the other hand, is rather opposed to joining up."

This pulls Adrian's attention away from the broad. "We've been through this, Uncle George," he seethes.

Our server returns to drop off a basket of bread. George snaps up a piece.

"Yes, we have," George confirms. He fiddles with a butter packet. "Adrian is a bit of a peacenik—won't fight the Enemy, won't even fight the Heretics."

"Uncle George…"

He looks at me with pleading eyes. "I just wish the boy would consider it."

"Uncle George, don't talk about me in the third person when I'm sitting next to you."

"You know it was so good of you boys to come out and have lunch with me," says George, brushing the complaint aside. He loosens the collar of his white and gray shirt—the white is cotton, the gray is scattered patches of sweat working in conjunction with the cotton. "It's warm in here, isn't it?"

I nod slightly. My mind has wandered to Kira. I hope the date goes well. It has to go well. I've felt so lost in this place. Maybe she can help me work things out.

George turns to Adrian. "Claire tells me you have a concert."

"Yeah, at the Red Lion."

"What's that?"

My friend winces. "It's a rock club on the boardwalk."

"A what? Don't mumble! You have to speak up."

Adrian practically yells, "It's a rock club on the boardwalk!"

"Oh, rock 'n roll. That is 'all the rage' these days, isn't it?" George says, making quotes with his fingers. Adrian winces again. "Is it a new concert hall, then?"

"No, it's been there for about fifteen years now."

"That sounds pretty new to me."

Adrian smiles weakly.

"You know, this bread is really hard," George says with evident irritation. "Is Seven going?"

"Yes, and he's got a date!" The strength of Adrian's expression increases dramatically.

"You have a date, Seven?! Fast work, my boy! Ho ho!"

I smile weakly.

"You know, Adrian, I used to take your great aunt to concerts. She loved the opera." George beams at the memory. "I never cared for it, really."

●

"I can't stand him," Adrian says to me, waving a final goodbye to George outside the restaurant. "He's living in the past."

"He certainly has fond memories."

"And that's all he has. In his head, the Great War never ended. Everything is about him fighting the Heretics. It's all he talks about."

"Yeah."

"I mean, he's good for a free lunch every now and then, but sometimes it's not even worth the stress. He's just too goddamned old to relate to about anything!"

Adrian lets loose a short, exasperated yell before concluding, "It will be good to just get back to the store."

"How did he—?" I try to find the words. "How did he take what happened to your dad?"

Adrian glances sideways at me. "I don't know. I think he's in denial. Knowing him, he'd want to take the side of the government. He always puts the Guard over his family. Always. I'm lucky he hasn't tried to turn me in for something."

"You think he'd do that?"

"I'm sure he could if he tried. It'd be something really stupid. But you know, truly 'pure' citizens, or whatever they're calling them..." he trails off. "People like that are pretty rare these days. The Guard could probably get something on my grandmother if they were bored enough.

"But c'mon," he says, "enough about that shit. Ready for that date tonight?"

Every time someone reminds me I've got a date with Kira, I feel a sharp pain in my heart. "I'm a little nervous," I admit. "But I should be okay once I see her."

"She's hot, man. You really lucked out with that one. Do you know how many times I've come into work dreaming that something like that would happen to me? Then you show up to work, your first fucking day, and a pretty girl practically jumps into your arms. Don't get me wrong, I'm happy for you dude, but that is such total bullshit!"

I shrug him off with a smile. "What can I say?"

Adrian slaps me on the back, bends in close and whispers, "Why don't you just shut up?"

10
METRO

A 20-something guy with a blond ponytail and white track jacket is pacing about the platform and whistling like an idiot. He has an extraordinary sense of pitch and an amazing lack of shame. He presses the pause button every now and then to spit on the track.

I drop a circular white mint into my mouth.

"If you see someone leave a bag," an automated voice is saying, "kindly ask them, 'Is that your bag?' If it's not theirs, please alert the station security center immediately. We value your help in keeping Metro safe."

A woman in a gray business suit lifts her wrist yet again to read her watch. Her other hand, clutching a briefcase, is bone white.

The station clock reads *8:32 p.m.* I'll probably get to the boardwalk early, but that's better than being late.

The lights along the track begin to blink on and off. The train arrives. The woman with the wristwatch pushes into the car before anyone has a chance to get off. I do the polite thing and wait. The whistler doesn't get on, but he stares through the window until we start moving.

I drop another mint, feel my tongue tingle. I wonder if I'll kiss her tonight.

"—that down on Irving?" chirps one of the passengers.

"Kind of," says the girl clinging to his arm. "It's like...you know where Good Time Records is?"

"Vaguely."

"You know, down near the Green Lounge."

"Oh!" he bursts. "I've had some crazy nights there. That's— that's on Rossdale!"

"Yeah, so if you go down Rossdale a little ways, there's a gas station, and then if you go down a little bit further, well, there it is."

"Oh all right!" he smiles. "I'll have to head down there some time."

Dance music blasts through the headphones of the quite-possibly-deaf kid in front of me. I pop another mint and stare at the subway map. I can't concentrate long enough to figure out my route. The locomotive screeches and squeals against the cold metal rails.

A graffiti image of the jet black figure with fire in his eyes, same as the one on Adrian's card and at the cemetery Monorail station, is painted on the back of the hearing-loss patient's seat. I gaze up at the ad for National University. The textbook in the busty, short skirt-wearing girl's arms says *Physics*. Didn't notice that the first time.

I wonder where National University is located, exactly. Science must be its specialty or something. No wait, then they'd call it an institute of technology, right? Probably, it's just a liberal arts school. I dunno, whatever.

The heat of a stranger's eyes sears into me. He smells a strange mix of sweat, whiskey and cheap cologne. Is he drunk? It's not even nine!

Damn it, I'm going to be so early.

●

Another prolonged metallic cry as the train comes to a halt. I still have a few more stops to go. Several people exit, including the kid with the oversized headphones.

Two Guard step aboard. Neither takes a seat; instead they seize the pole near the door. They gaze blankly out opposite windows. Somewhat illogically, I check to see if either of their faces matches the one that accosted Adrian and me the other night. All the Guard look about the same—clean-shaven and muscular—but I don't think I've seen these soldiers before.

"So how's Marie?" one Guard asks the other.

"Oh you know," Guard B responds. "She wants me home more—doesn't really understand."

"Right," says Guard A.

Guard B cuts back in, "Don't get me wrong, I love the old girl to death."

"Yeah, know how you feel. Comes with the territory."

"No getting around it."

I can't believe I'm meeting this girl for a date. Something about the way I set that up with her was too easy. Dammit, I've already discussed this in my head, haven't I? Chill, Seven. Just take things as they come. Wait—discussed in my head? Damn, if someone could read my thoughts, they'd probably diagnose me with acute schizophrenia. I'm like a crazy person.

"You should have seen this Heretic today," Guard A laughs. "He's just walkin' down the street, wearin' a sign that says *Free the People*! I go up and I say 'Now sir, just what is that supposed to mean? And you know what he says?"

"What?"

"He says some shit about our country being doomed, how the Enemy is gonna come blow us up...and then, and then, he goes, 'Sir, we are all prisoners!'"

"You serious? God. Fucking loony."

"You said it, man, you said it," Guard A chuckles. "So you know what I say? I'm like 'Not yet, citizen, but you just wait a few minutes!'"

"Hah!" Guard B exclaims. "Well played!"

•

The train slows and the doors slide. A voice coming from the speaker announces, "Fairview." The soldiers exit the train along with a throng of citizens. Still not my stop. I glance at the map again, biting hard into my latest mint. Shit, I'm *definitely* going to be early.

"Hey....kid...what in God's name are you...so nervous 'bout?" I follow the slurred voice to the scraggly, unshaven mouth of the drunk.

"Oh…I'm just…new in town… not used to the Metro yet."

"Thas' a likely story….I know kids these days—you're up to somethin'!" He glares menacingly into my eyes.

What? "No, I—"

"D'ya…d'ya know what we do to Heretics…young man?"

"I'm not a…" My head swivels around the car, searching for an escape.

Oh my God, are we the only ones left in this fucking car? My hand claws at the hard plastic seat.

He flashes a half-toothed grin and then sneers, "Dropped! We have 'em dropped, we have 'em dropped, dropped, dropped! D'ya want to be dropped, young…man?"

"Look, I haven't done anything wrong."

The slight tinge of antagonism in my voice widens the man's yellow-glazed eyes. "And ya not gonna, Heretic."

There's a flick and a light from his hand blinds me—he's got a switchblade.

"No," I whimper. "Stop."

The maniac jumps me. I dodge to my left and trip him.

"Son of a—" he groans, struggling to his feet.

I kick him upside the chin, sending him flailing onto his back.

He groans, and then says no more. I stare.

●

The speaker announces, "Boardwalk." I dart off the train, eyes to the floor, past a whining group of people. Halfway up the escalator, I hear a scream from the train. It's followed by a melodic ding-dong and a recording that sings, "Doors closing!"

11
LOVE & HATE

I lean against the railing, close my eyes and take a deep breath. The air is chewy with cotton candy. My eyes open and take in a star-speckled sky. Boardwalk lights cast a shimmer in the water that's almost too magnificent to put into words. And the long row of restaurants, carnival games and cheap stores make the throngs of pedestrians glow neon.

"Hello there."

It's her! I turn around and smile, "Hey. How's it going?"

"It's going good, how are you?"

"Can't complain," I answer. Kira looks amazing—crimson blouse, short black skirt...how the hell did I set up a date with her?

I realize I should say something. "So...dinner..."

"There's a pretty good pizza place a few blocks down this way..." She points with her finger.

"All right, sounds like a plan." Commence strolling. "It's a really nice night, isn't it?"

"Yeah, definitely," Kira smiles. "We lucked out."

"So, uh..."

She turns her head slightly in my direction and I nearly trip. Finally, I think of something to talk about.

"How was your day?"

She breathes a quick laugh, "It was all right, I guess."

"What do you do, anyway?"

Kira pauses for a moment as if unsure how to answer, which

makes me more nervous. "Well, currently I wait tables, but I'm attending law school."

"You're gonna be a lawyer?"

"Yes, if I play my cards right...a prosecutor."

My eyebrows rise slightly.

Kira's voice quickens, "So what's it like working at a bookstore?"

"Kind of boring, actually. I basically sit and read all day."

She nods slightly.

"But I mean, it does have its good sides."

She smiles again, looks away and whispers: "Yeah, I suppose it does."

"It's temporary, really," I say. "I have to, you know, figure a few things out." This is awful.

Up ahead, I see a small red rollercoaster, lit up for the night. "Want to ride?" I say.

She gives me a strange look.

"—On the roller coaster," I stammer, "—over there."

"Oh!" She slaps her head lightly and mutters a bit to herself. Then she exclaims, "Yeah, let's go!"

"All right, and then we can get something to eat afterward. I figure it wouldn't be a good idea to do it the other way around!"

Kira chuckles and lowers her voice to say, "Nooo, no it wouldn't." Then she exclaims, "Hey, I'll race you!"

"You're on." We line up behind one of the walk's wooden planks.

"Ready...set..." She pauses for dramatic effect. "Go!"

We take off down the boardwalk, getting confused looks from passersby. Kira is surprisingly fast, and it takes every ounce of my strength to catch up to her. Just as I draw close, she throws her arm out and pushes back ahead across the imaginary finish line.

"Hey, wait a minute!" I protest.

"Yeah! Take that!" she laughs.

"Very nice, young lady," comments a gruff-voiced and overall sketchy old man. Startled, Kira and I spin in his direction. "Want a ride on the roller coaster?"

Carnies. I hand him the money and we get in a two-seater. I've barely got my belt on when the train starts its slow, rickety ascent. "I always hate this part," Kira says.

I place my hand lightly over hers. "Scared?"

"Shut up," she laughs, grasping my hand and squeezing it.

Soon we've reached the peak. "Here it comes…"

The girl screams in ecstasy. My troubles explode and fall away.

•

I suck on my soda straw and get nothing but air.

"You know I've always loved coming to this beach," Kira beams, carefully placing the crust of her latest pizza slice next to two others on her paper plate. "My dad used to bring me here all the time—he loved the water. We'd get here and he'd run in—just like a little kid—only he'd pull me along, too."

"Not as big a fan?" I offer.

"It was cold! Always! And this one time, I'd just seen a shark movie the night before!"

"Aw, poor little Kira."

"Hey shut up, I bet you were the same way."

"I honestly can't remember."

"Hah, yeah right."

"So if you were so scared of the water, why did you love coming here so much?"

"Good question," Kira laughs. "No, I guess it was more just seeing Daddy so happy…and then the boardwalk was great, of course—all those rides." She looks at me—no, gazes at me. The roller coaster idea was a winner, I s'pose.

I ask, "What does your dad do?"

"He's a priest," she smiles, kicking my foot lightly under the table.

"A priest, really?" I spit out. "So you must be pretty religious?"

I feel her foot move away. "No more than the next girl."

I give the straw another bite. "Okay," I try to conclude.

"Why do you ask?"

"Oh," I stutter, "Well, I was just wondering, because I mean, I figure if you have, like, such a religious, um, figure—you know—so prominently in your life—your dad—things might be a little different, maybe?"

"I guess," she says. "Never really thought about it like that."

She starts playing with one of her discarded pizza crusts. I glance at my watch.

"How much time do we have before the show?" she asks.

"Uh," I begin, and then look at my watch again. "Well, ten minutes for doors."

"Didn't you just read the time?" she asks slyly.

"Sorry?"

"You just looked at your watch, didn't you?"

"Oh, yeah, I do that sometimes," I stammer. "Pretty girls make me nervous."

She leans back in her chair and laughs. "Oh, do they?"

"Check?" a voice interrupts. Our waiter has just emerged out of nowhere.

"Sure," I tell him. When he walks away, I whisper to Kira, "Where did that guy even come from?"

"I don't know, but I hate when people are sneaky like that."

"I'll keep that in mind," I say.

Kira laughs, brushes her shoe against my ankle.

●

Wisps of cigarette smoke drift and curl above our heads. Bass blasts punch at a hundred people talking at once. Kira says she thinks the mix tape they got on is horrible, but as I watch her eyes roll I feel completely at peace.

We got here a bit early, but at least it gave us the opportunity to get a spot by the stage, right in front of the microphone stand. Hell, the set list is right there in front of me. Now I know what they're gonna play before anyone else does. Don't I feel special?

I can't help but admire the guitar on the stage—probably Adrian's. It has a classic shape and a black finish. The way it rests in its stand throws me into a state of awe.

Incidentally, Kira is so hot. How the hell did I find a girl like this? And the way she looks at me! If there weren't so many people around, I might just make out with her right here.

I turn away from Kira's brilliant blue eyes for a second to gaze at the mezzanine level behind me. There's some seats up there, but most of the people lean over the railing. I must have been to a few of these shows before, because I understand their mentality: it's easier to rock out standing up. The pain in your knees disappears once you're entranced.

"God, why do they play such shit music before concerts all the time?" Kira asks again. She probably just wants to talk. What's a good conversation starter?

"So have you seen this band before?" I ask.

"No, but I've heard good things."

"We can probably go backstage after their set."

"Really?" Kira smiles. "Yeah, okay."

Nice one, Seven. Smooth.

It's awesome to hear Adrian has a good reputation. I've only known him for a few days but I can't help but root for him. He's just been an overall good guy...couldn't have asked for a better person to help me through my situation. Fuck, without that dude, I wouldn't have this hot babe in my arms, now would I?

Kira's smiling like a kid about to open her first birthday present. "You know, I don't think there's going to be an opening band tonight," she says.

I nod. A faint whiff of marijuana in my nostrils suddenly and strangely reminds me to ask her if she wants a drink. She does.

I push past a few teenagers in tattered black denim and find a clearing at the bar. I order the drinks and glance back in Kira's direction. She looks me in the eyes and my heart leaps. I smile awkwardly and turn back to the bartender.

As I wait for the beers, someone waves a fistful of money in the bartender's face. The customer grunts a thank you and grabs a bottle of lager from the counter. Mechanically, he turns. I take in the cold, steely glare and choke back a gasp—I know him. Last night, he paid the hostel a visit. Tonight, he's here to watch Adrian.

"Sir?" the bartender prompts me tiredly.

I trade him the rest of my allowance. There goes the notion of me giving Adrian back some change.

I look around for the watchman, but he's vanished into the crowd. I pick up the drinks and return to my gorgeous date.

Kira grabs a pint from my hand. "The band should be coming on soon," she says.

I take a sip and pat her on the shoulders lightly. "You just can't wait, can you?"

"What can I say?" she laughs, sticking her tongue out for a moment. "I love this stuff."

I kiss her as the lights dim. The techno music is replaced by the voracious buzz of the audience. The cheering gets absolutely thunderous when Adrian, Ron and Jake stroll on stage. There's no "hello." The band picks up their instruments and the storm begins.

"As the sky catches fire…" Adrian sings.

Kira leans back in my arms. My heart beats to the rhythm of the drum.

"…in your eyes, forever apart!"

Adrian breaks into a soaring guitar solo and Kira clasps my hand in hers. Red and yellow lights wash over us.

"It's too late for us now…"

I close my eyes for a few seconds, reopen them slowly.

"…it's too late for us now, too late, too late…"

A heavily distorted bass riff from Ron, but Adrian's guitar breaks through. And then with a cymbal crash it's all over.

"Good evening, friends," the singer booms.

We roar in response.

"Thanks for coming out. We're called Beacon."

Jake, suddenly shirtless, clicks his drumsticks and shouts "One, two, three, four!" Ron launches into a heavy groove. A drum fill later and Adrian's jagged guitar cuts in.

Ron is yelling maniacally.

Kira is warm in my hands. She half-turns her head, smiling mischievously.

The guitar carries me away. Before I know it, the song has ended and Adrian is grabbing an acoustic guitar from offstage. He plays a haunting introduction and then the drums and bass join the slow, exploring melody.

"I'm lying in bed. The music's put me in a trance and the ceiling fan spins and spins and things don't feel the same anymore. I'm lost but won't stop. I'll keep on going till I'm found..."

She's so soft.

"Blacking out the sunrise..."

Kira shifts my hand up to her breasts. Oh my God. The crowd roars its appreciation, and I haven't enough hands to clap. Adrian looks over at me and winks.

"Thank you all so much. This next song is about living in fucked up times." Adrian takes a sip of his beer. "They took my parents. Don't let them take you."

The audience roars. Kira stiffens.

"You okay?" I ask. She doesn't hear me.

Adrian reaches off the side of the stage again to get his electric guitar back. He starts playing arpeggio on the high strings.

"Boy on a train wearing headphones, looking for melody in the distortion. He's surrounded by dystrophy, keeps searching for warm light under the shadow. On and on and on into the darkness! Fade away with me..."

Something red appears in the center of Adrian's forehead.

"Hey, do you see—?" I yell into Kira's ear.

The microphone amplifies the thunk of the bullet. The guitar cries out in dissonance. Ron and Jake glance over confusedly. Adrian grimaces, lets go of his instrument. The weight pulls him down by the neck and into the scuffed black stage floor, creating another loud electric bang. The crowd screams. Jake gapes. Ron unplugs his bass guitar and runs off stage. The panicked faces obscure my vision. I watch a woman fall over and disappear.

"Seven!" Kira yells, pulling me forcefully toward the stage. "This way!" She jumps up and runs off. I start to follow but can't continue. Adrian's crumpled on the floor, unmoving. And up on the mezzanine is the steely-eyed murderer. He leans over the railing, dangles his gun lazily, watches the mayhem like a vulture.

I tear back through the crowd. I'm ignited and the fire spreads with each step. I come face to face with the demon, a cell phone pressed against his cold white face. The flames consume me. My fist crashes into the phone, embedding its black plastic splinters into the man's ear. He howls. His thick knee slams into my stomach and suddenly I'm back against the mezzanine railing, wheezing furiously. He jumps at me and begins to bend me over the fence. The odor of cheap beer invades my nostrils.

I grab a bottle and break it against the side of his head. His eyes widen. Now I stab what's left of it into his face.

He staggers back. Soon my hands are tight around his neck and I push him into the floor. His arms are pinned underneath my knees. His eyes bulge crimson. He stops struggling.

First I take his gun, and then I pull a wallet out of his pocket. The ID reads *Mr. Doug Smith, Elite Guard*. I stuff it into my jeans, get up and move for the stairs.

A bubbly cough—I whirl around and fire twice into the murderer's forehead. He twitches like an upturned beetle.

"Seven?!" Kira yells in the distance. She's waiting for me back on the stage, unaware. I run to her, grab her by the hand. We find a fire door backstage and set off an alarm pushing our way out. The dirty brick walls float by; the street lights gleam cold in the night.

We run forever. We collapse on a bench.

"You're covered with blood!" Kira yelps.

I say nothing. We stare into the distance.

"He's dead," I manage at last.

"I'm so sorry, Seven. Adrian slipped up."

I almost slap her, but resist. "—What?!"

"He must have been on the Watched List. No one on that list lives for very long." I feel Kira's eyes on me. "Are you okay?"

I hear myself breathe in and out, in and out.

She looks at my hand; it still clasps the revolver of Mr. Doug Smith, Elite Guard. "Oh my God…. Seven?!"

"He's dead," I say again, salt water tears dripping into my gaping mouth.

●

The tip of the pistol that shot Adrian and Mr. Doug Smith pokes out from my crumpled jacket. I can't go back to the hostel. I can't go back to the bookstore. And Kira shouldn't let me stay with her.

For the past few minutes my host has been rattling and clinking away in the kitchen. She's got a nice place—a big, well-decorated, one-bedroom apartment. The paintings of sailing ships at sea are bland, yet somehow comforting.

"Here you are, Seven," Kira says daintily, handing me a sparkling crystal glass of red. She pushes my jacket aside and sits beside me on the sofa carefully. I give the glass a little shake and watch the liquid swirl.

"We cannot allow the Heretics to get away with senseless murder," announces the television, which is to say President Drake.

"I'll be right back," whispers Kira, retreating to her bedroom.

"Our unity cannot be weakened by internal deviants. It is my solemn promise to increase the power of the recently formed Department of Purity in order to tighten unity at home. The Guard will be strengthened. We will hunt down and destroy the Heretics."

I lay back on the sofa for a minute. When I raise my head again, a reporter is talking. "A great cleansing has begun." He flashes a desolate and cadaverous grin at the camera.

I fumble for the remote, change the channel. Another maniacal reporter, this one in a trench coat, stands in front of the Capitol Tower, the wind rustling just the tips of his well-kept hair. He reminds me of Adrian's killer.

"Doug Smith is the second Elite Guard to be killed by Heretics in two weeks," he says. "If you remember, Jane, last week Agent Jonathan Wyle disappeared while on a separate assignment to stop the spread of Heresy. It's assumed he too was victim of what the President is now calling a 'slowly spreading virus.'"

Where's Kira? I need her to come back.

The image flickers into a newsroom where a glamorous blonde gasps in terror. "Horrible! Dave, do the Guard have a suspect?"

"I've been assured that they are pursuing him as we speak."

I click the remote and it's the video of the President again, an awful sneer on his face. "—hunt down and destroy the Heretics."

I tear away from the screen. I need to find Kira.

The door to her bedroom is shut. "Yes," Kira says from the other side. "He's here."

I nearly drop my drink.

"Yes," she says, "I will."

I'm back in the living room, grabbing at my coat. The TV reporters yap away.

This can't…she can't…

The gun tumbles out of the pocket. Frantically, I pick it up and shove it back inside.

Why would she…?

I'm out the door.

I'm down the stairs.

I'm on the street.

I cut through a dank alleyway and run until all I can hear is my own heavy breathing.

12
COCKROACH

Something is scratching against my neck.

"A dead guy!" a child's voice bursts jubilantly.

"Sarah! Get away from that lowlife and put the stick down!" a woman's voice scolds.

My eyes open slowly, let the sunlight in ray by ray. I'm next to a metal trash can on the edge of an alleyway. I see the woman and her daughter's backs as they accelerate away, the mother's hand clamped firmly around the girl's arm. I close my eyes and see Adrian letting go of his guitar and keeling forward.

I vomit a smelly mess onto the cracked asphalt.

Why didn't the Guard find me here? Maybe they know less about me than I feared. No, they must have talked to Kira. She could describe me to them—she wants to be a fucking prosecutor!

Why would she turn me in? We were getting along so well! I thought maybe I could trust her.

What, after one date? Idiot.

No, but the date went so well.

Maybe she's just easy. Ever think of that, jackass?

I knock the trash can over as I rise to my feet. The clang is immensely satisfying.

Does Claire know already? Who's going to be the one to tell her Adrian is dead—the Guard? They already took away her child; now they've murdered her grandson. I wish I could go and talk to her myself. But the Guard might have an ID on me by now. They've likely got the hostel on priority watch. I have to lie low.

So where am I going to go?

An aroma of grilled food answers my question. I ride the pleasing scent out of the alleyway like a cartoon dog. Soon I'm standing outside a small pub with a sign that reads *Blackbird Arms*.

I'll go in, get a burger, maybe a soda. I'll get myself sorted once my stomach's satisfied.

I pull out Mr. Doug Smith's wallet to see how realistic the plan is. There's a nice little wad—at least a hundred—finally, a little luck!

●

Hungrily, I pull open the tavern's heavy wood door. I'm hit by a blast of vintage rock. Adrian lets go of his guitar.

"Somethin' ta drink?" the bartender asks. He's a rather tan man, balding a little on top and looking a bit pudgy in a grease-stained blue polo shirt.

"Yeah, well, actually, do you have anything to eat?"

"We got menus on the tables," he sneers.

"Oh, right, thanks." I rise from the bar stool and grab one.

"Put that back when you're done," he tells me.

I order a half-pound burger, topped with bacon and smothered with grilled onions. I also get a cola and some fries. Just communicating words like "bacon" and "fries" makes me salivate, and I have to wipe my mouth mid-request.

"Are you going to put that back?" the bartender asks, indicating the menu I've let drop on the bar.

"Oh," I jump out of my seat. "Yeah, sorry."

I was really starting to like Kira. She had this vibrancy, like a kid, but not in a creepy way. And everything was going so well. God, imagine what might have happened if things had gone differently last night.

Shut up, Seven—your only real friend is dead and the girl betrayed you. Get a fucking grip.

Well, at least I woke up with some memory this time.

Yeah—fun, useful memories you have.

Indeed. So, what's taking this burger so long?

Shut up, it's barely been a minute!

I continue to psychotically argue with myself until a warm and extremely appealing sandwich is miraculously placed under my nose. I tear into the meat and its delicious juice runs down my chin.

Out of the corner of my eye I note a pair of elderly women gawking at me from their booth. One's shaking her head. I turn— they turn away.

Oh, whatever. I dip into the fries, take the straw out of the soda and practically chug it.

"Hey Joe," a skinny man in a white-collared shirt greets the bartender. He takes a seat two stools away. What's left of his graying hair looks like it's been tugged at.

"Hi, Bruce. How's things with you?"

"Not bad, not bad," he says, eyes shifting nervously to the bar. "Well—not good actually. Walt's missing. He didn't come home for dinner last week, and we haven't seen or heard from him since."

"Well you know kids," the bartender trails off absent-mindedly.

Bruce looks up again, frantically. "Not Walt though. Walt is a good boy, Joe. He'd never run away, not Walt! It's like he's disappeared. I went to the police—they said they didn't know anything—said if something had happened to him they'd have a report—and, and I checked—there wasn't a report—nothing about Walt!"

"Well, that's good, ain't it?"

"I s'pose so, but I just..."

Walt...where have I heard that name before? I take a long sip of my soda. Instead of an answer, my own problems re-invade my mind.

The bartender frowns. "He'll turn up, Bruce. Walt's a good kid, just like you said. How about something to drink?"

"Uh, sure—all—all right. I'll have a beer—no, make it whiskey—straight."

•

Two-thirds of the burger is polished off, and I'm beginning to feel guilty. I'm eating like I haven't a care in the world.

"Have you recently experienced injury due to poor medical

care?" the radio booms. "My name is Nick Dimacello and I can get you money! Call me right now at 62-8329-642. That's 62-8329-642. I only make money when you get the reward you deserve! Call me right this instant! That number again is 62-8329-642! Call me now! My name is Nick Dimacello! Call now and get money!"

Another phone number jolts my memory: The rebels.

I flag the bartender down. "You got a phone in here?"

"Yeah, in the back, by the toilet," he points past the old bags in the booth.

"Great, thanks. This was delicious, by the way."

The compliment seems to puzzle him more than anything else, but he manages a "Yer welcome."

I shove the last morsel into my mouth, sit back to let my stomach recuperate. The check comes crashing down in front of me. I fork over some of Mr. Doug Smith's dough.

•

Taking a deep breath, I slide shut the phone booth door.

What was the name of the girl on the card? Annie? Anne....Ana! That's it!

I dial the number. As it rings, I notice a stack of newspapers beside the booth. The main headline reads in big bold letters: *President Drake Calls for State Cleansing.*

Then, a slightly garbled feminine voice greets "Hello?"

"Hi, is Ana there?"

"Speaking, who's this?"

My heart pounds.

"Hello?"

"This is Adrian. You left your card the other night."

"Adrian?" The phone goes dead. Then it comes back to life. "Oh! Hey! How come you waited so long?"

"Er," I stutter. Adrian was such an idiot; she sounds hot, too. "I'm a bit...disorganized," I say at last. "—didn't realize I had your number until recently."

"Sorry I had to cut out on you so early, babe."

"It's fine." I gotta change the subject. "I'm kind of in a bit of trouble right now...with the Guard."

"And you're calling me?"

"Well," I stammer, "I mean the picture on your card, it—"

"Shut up! Where are you?"

"A pub...the Blackbird Arms."

"Is that on Stockwood?"

"Uh, I forget, never been here before—I just kind of wandered in, I guess."

"Aw, that's cute," she purrs. "I'll be right over, sweetie. Get us a table."

The phone clicks before I can reply.

●

I grab a newspaper on the way back to the bar.

"Thanks for comin' in, sir," the bartender welcomes me back.

"Sure," I reply, hesitating until he turns away to add, "Actually, can I get a table?"

He looks back, obviously perplexed.

"I'm...I'm meeting someone here."

"But you already ate."

Son of a bitch. "I didn't know she was coming."

Still baffled, he waves at the tables. "Sit wherever you want."

I go for a nice booth in the back corner. It doesn't take long for a waitress to accost me.

"Something to drink?" she chirps.

"Uh, actually I'm just waiting for someone right now."

"Something while you wait?"

"No thanks."

"Sir, only paying customers are really supposed to—"

"I just bought a whole meal at the bar!" I practically yell.

The bartender looks over, and the waitress flashes him a confused and somewhat concerned look, much like a kitten just told to get off the goddamned dinner table. His fingers make an okay sign.

The waitress' voice returns to its original, overly enthusiastic tone: "Righty-o!" Then she starts skipping off toward the kitchen.

"Wait," I bleat. "You have a mint or something?"

"One second, darling," she shoots back.

I unfold the newspaper and spread it over the table.

President William T. Drake last night outlined a plan to tighten control over the state and rid our great nation of Heresy once and for all. The decision came shortly after police found the body of Elite Guard Doug Smith at the Red Lion rock club.

"Our unity cannot be weakened by internal deviants," said President Drake. "It is my solemn promise to increase the power of the recently formed Department of Purity in order to tighten unity at home."

Drake said the "slowly spreading virus" of Heresy has grown in recent years. Not acting now could mean another crisis like the one 40 years ago in the Great War, he added.

Smith was found dead on the mezzanine level of the Red Lion during a concert for local band Beacon. Police said he was strangled and then shot twice in the head.

"I think there was a gunshot or something. Everyone was screaming," said Richard Berry, 18. "I guess a Heretic must have spotted the Guard and did the killing during the panic."

Doug Smith was the second Elite Guard to fall to the forces of Heresy this month. Last week, Agent Jonathan Wyle disappeared while on a separate assignment.

"A new chapter in our history has begun, but I believe it will be a short and sweet one," said President Drake. "When it's all over we won't have to worry about traitorous Heretic dogs ever again."

Nothing about Adrian. Then I see a small blurb about my friend in the bottom-left corner. The headline: *Rock Singer Wanted for Questioning*.

The leader of local rock band Beacon disappeared last night shortly after the murder of Elite Guard Doug Smith.

Adrian Bernard has not been seen since Guard found the mangled corpse of Smith resting on the mezzanine level of the Red Lion rock club.

Bernard vanished in the midst of a riot started by a previously unheard song. The tune, titled "Into the Darkness," contained lyrics encouraging Heresy, witnesses reported.

The Guard arrested Beacon bassist Ron Block and drummer

Jake Green at 12:35 a.m., but are still hunting Bernard, a spokesman said.

Bernard was the son of infamous traitor and Heretic Paul Bernard, who was executed after brutally killing a Guard six years ago.

So this is how they cover up a government-sponsored assassination. Nice of them to imply he might have killed his killer. On the plus side, these articles sort of indicate the Guard haven't identified me yet.

I start as something clatters onto the table.

"Your mint!" the waitress sings.

•

"Hi, I'm supposed to meet someone," says a gentle voice by the bar. "His name's Adrian."

I look up from the comics section. Ana is tall, slender and olive-skinned, with a trendy tortoiseshell glasses frame to match the hair. My mind goes blank—I forget my entire plan.

"That feller over there was waiting for someone," the bartender points in my direction. "Didn't tell me his name, though."

Ana looks over at me. "No, that's not…"

She trails off and furrows her brow because I've begun to wave and shout. "Ana! Over here!"

She makes a few unsure steps in my direction. "Are you a friend of Adrian's?"

"Yeah," I say, "I'm Seven."

"Funny name," she says blandly, scanning the room. "Where's Adrian?"

I flip the paper over and push it toward her, indicating the article about my friend.

"What's this?"

"Read it. I'm the one who called you—the one who's in trouble."

"So in other words, you don't know where he is either, huh?"

"He was murdered!" I choke on the word. "He was murdered by an Elite Guard."

Ana's head snaps up. "Keep it down!" she scolds, her jade eyes stabbing. "You can't just go around saying things like that. Do you even have any evidence?"

"I was there."

"Oh my God," Ana smiles. She leans in close and whispers, "You're the one they're after, aren't you?"

I hesitate for a moment, raise my finger in the air and start coughing uncontrollably.

"Clever boy... I wouldn't have come if I knew it was you on the other end of the line," Ana smirks, rising to her feet. "Well, good luck!"

I grab her by the wrist. "No, wait."

"Let go," she states with amazing calm.

I stare into her eyes and speak through my teeth, "I need your help."

"You need my help?" she practically laughs. "You're a liability! You could barely even keep your mouth shut on the phone!"

"You would have helped Adrian."

"You're not Adrian," she snaps.

"No, I'm not."

I pause. Damn, I should have planned for this, expected it. She pulls at her arm but my grip is too firm. What do I have that she might want? Money?

"Do you want me to scream for help?" she seethes. "I'll do it. I'll scream, and they'll add 'sexual predator' to your list of heretical sins."

No, she's not going to take money. But you do have his wallet.

"I've...I've got his wallet."

Ana's muscles relax and I let go. "Whose wallet?"

"*His* wallet," I say.

"Smith?" she whispers. "You have his ID?"

My heart leaps. "Yeah, I do."

Ana sits back down. "Show me it."

"What, right here? Isn't that a 'liability'?"

Ana stares at me for a few seconds, an expression of disbelief plastered to her face. "What do you want?"

"I want protection. I want help getting out of the Capital."

Ana gazes down at the table, shakes her head and mutters something incomprehensible.

"Welcome to the Blackbird Arms!" The waitress is back with a pad and pen in hand. "Can I get y'all something to drink?"

"No," Ana says without so much as turning her head to face the server.

"Sir?"

"I'm fine."

"Well, I can just bring out tap water," she says, frowning. "What would you like to eat?"

Ana doesn't say anything. Neither do I.

"Should I come back?"

"Yeah, come back," Ana says. The waitress walks away, shoulders hunched. Ana stares me cold in the eyes. "Fine! Whatever! Let's get out of here and we'll talk."

"Should we leave a tip?"

"Hell no. We didn't even get bread!"

13
HOLE

"Get in," Ana orders, whisking a fluffy white towel off the convertible's passenger seat and tossing it in the back. The seat is soft and creamy.

"Nice car," I vocalize. "You do pretty well for yourself, don't you?"

"Shut up," she answers. "I shouldn't be helping you. Don't make me change my mind."

"Sorry," I say. "Thank you."

The engine growls. We zoom off and the wind tears at my hair. She takes a hand off the steering wheel and reaches for a pack of cigarettes. Without taking her eyes off the road, Ana dips a stick into the vehicle's cigarette lighter and slides it in her mouth.

●

It's gotten overcast. There's a chill in the air, and being in a convertible doesn't help. We've barely gotten anywhere, but I can already tell Ana is a terrible driver. She keeps jerking around and loves to go fast—loves it so much she never brakes until the absolute last second. It takes every ounce of will power in my body to keep from yelling.

Be nice, man. You need her help.

"Watch it!" screams a pedestrian.

God damn it, this girl! We're in a quiet neighborhood of houses and small stores and she's trying to kill people. How much longer do I have to spend in this damn vehicle with this insane broad?

I wonder what kind of driver Kira is. Maybe she manages to avoid the stereotype.

•

Ana slows the convertible and flicks on the turn signal. The car behind us honks its horn. "Go around me, jerk!" she yells. Then she leans back in the chair and cranes her neck around.

Oh God, she's going to parallel park.

Ana shifts her automatic into reverse, turns the wheel all the way to the right, and releases the brake pedal. Then she slams it and starts spinning the wheel the other way.

"What are we doing here?" I ask at last. Around us is a bank, a pharmacy and a grocery store—we're still in the middle of a residential area.

"The best hiding places are right out in the open," she smiles. "Am I close enough to the curb?"

It's obvious that we're not, but I push open my door anyway. The space is large enough to fit a motorcycle—comfortably. "No," I say.

"Fuck." Ana shifts into drive and moves forward. Then she twists the wheel right and goes back into reverse. We edge forward and slightly more to the right. "Now?"

"Well, it's an improvement," I offer.

Ana shifts into park, unbuckles her seatbelt, and leans over my legs to inspect the gap. Her hair gets in my face and her shoulder rubs slightly against my chest. "Eh," she says. "I've seen worse." She pushes against my legs to boost herself back into her own seat. I unbuckle and roll out.

Ana closes the roof and locks up the vehicle. She clutches a purse with one hand and motions to me with the other. "All right, let's go." She moves for the bank called DAY.

"Need to cash a check?"

"Smartass," she remarks, sliding a card to unlock the door.

We come upon another set of doors, but the bank is closed. No matter, though—Ana moves for the ATM machine on the right. She slides the card once more.

"Should I look the other way?"

She laughs. "It's not like I'm getting undressed."

Ana taps in a needlessly lengthy PIN number. "Good lord that's long," I say.

"That's what she said."

She hits enter. The ATM machine slides up into the ceiling, revealing a dark passageway. "Ta daaa!" she announces with a lift of the arms.

"Oh," I offer. "Um, after you."

"Why thank you, darling."

•

The secret door comes back down, leaving us in near darkness. "Now don't get any ideas," she purrs.

Adrian's "best sex in his life" claim pops into my head. It's hard to decide if Ana is flirting with me or if that's just her natural way. I try to shake the feeling aside, and follow the sound of her footsteps.

Ana stops suddenly. She knocks on a door I can't quite find. After three hits she shouts, "Open up, David!"

"Quiet, girl. Someone might be withdrawing cash and hear you," scolds a somewhat husky, somewhat squeaky voice on the other side. There's a click and I have to shield my eyes from the light. I squint and blink a few times at a black man in jeans and a white muscle shirt.

"New boyfriend?" he smirks.

"Fuck you," she laughs. "He's got something for us."

"Uh, hi," I say, my eyes still adjusting. The space is literally a hole in the wall—windowless and crowded with crude, dirt-encrusted technology. There are a couple doorways in the back, but it's basically a box. Florescent lights hum overhead.

"Who is he?" David asks her, all the humor from the last interchange gone.

"His name is Seven. He says he has an Elite Guard's ID."

"Says he has an Elite Guard ID?" David repeats. He takes a deep breath. "Girl, we can't just bring home every stranger who claims to have a fucking ID! The bastard could be a fucking Elite Guard, himself!"

"No, he actually killed one," Ana answers, but this just creates more alarm on David's face. "And he doesn't claim," she stammers. "He has it—I saw it."

That's of course a lie, but I decide not to call her out on it. We're not exactly chums yet.

"Whoa, back up, back up! You mean to tell me this is the urchin from the Red Lion last night?"

"That's what he says."

David gapes at me. "Damn, boy!" And then to Ana: "Well, you still shouldn't have brought him here. He could have given it to you on the outside."

"I couldn't do that," I cut in. "I need protection…the Underground's protection. I need to get out of the Capital."

"You're going to need to go a hell of a lot further than that if you killed an Elite, boy."

"Look, I don't have a lot of options. I just need somewhere to stay until I can get things together and find a way out."

"What does this look like, a fucking hotel?"

"I don't need much," I say with slight stutter. "I'll take whatever you've got."

He glares, and then growls: "Give me the card. If it checks out, you've got your goddamned protection."

I hold out Mr. Doug Smith's ID card and David yanks it away.

"But you fucking better follow our laws in the meantime."

"Laws?"

"I'm sorry, allow me to elaborate," he sneers sarcastically. "You may not leave here unless I give you *permission*. We will bring you food and provide you with a bed—"

I gasp. "There's a bed in here?"

Ana points to a dirt-encrusted doorway in the back corner. "In there. It's kind of, um, squeaky."

"I'm sure it will do." I force a smile at David, who's still scowling.

"Me, Ana and Eric—he'll be here in a bit—don't spend nights here. We have our own apartments. I'm going to lock you in when we're not around—for your own protection."

"It's just the three of you, then?"

"Since last week, yes."

I decide not to request another elaboration. Instead, I ask what they're going to do with Mr. Doug Smith's ID card.

"I don't have time to explain that to you." David ditches Ana and me for a computer.

Ana smiles awkwardly. "The card contains a microchip containing the agent's profile and mission information," she says. "They do it in case the agent goes down. It helps them form a list of suspects and uh, arrange the funeral faster."

"Seven—get over here," David commands.

Maybe he wants to show me a few things about the man I killed?

But the computer screen isn't displaying anything about Mr. Doug Smith at all. It just reads *Waiting for scan*. David shoves a plastic, dirt-encrusted pad in my direction. It's connected to the wall with a coiled telephone wire, yellowed with age—they might have got it from a garage sale.

"Put your hand on it," David barks.

I feel a slight buzz. Then David pulls the device away, slaps it on the table and begins click-clacking on a stained keyboard. Grunting, he waves me away.

I turn to see Ana's hands playing with her hair. She stares at me blankly.

"What did he just do?" I ask.

She comes out of the daze with some annoyance. "We have to confirm you are who you say you are, and not who you say you aren't."

"What?"

She sighs. "We're checking with HQ to make sure you're not fucking with us."

"How long will that take?"

She rolls her eyes and exhales, "Five, ten minutes?"

"Where's HQ?"

"In the land of Fuck Off!" David yells from his post.

"Hey, be nice," Ana scolds.

There's a sudden rapping at the door. David and Ana turn fast. "Open up, Heretics!"

They've found me.

Ana chuckles, moseys toward the door and pulls it open. "For fuck's sake, Eric."

"Hey babe." A freckled twenty-something jock walks in. His hair is short and astoundingly red. Ana jumps into his arms, smooches him, and then points in my direction. "Eric? Seven," she says. "Seven? Eric. Seven's going to be staying with us for a little while, babe."

Eric nods in my direction, but his sharp blue eyes soon resume their gaze on Ana. "You can tell me all about it later, babe."

I turn wide-eyed and open mouthed to David, but his eyes remain fixed on the computer. Eric and Ana kiss again. I smile somewhat bitterly and excuse myself—now might be a good time to check out my room.

●

The large brown stain on the mattress is the first thing I notice. I toss my coat at it, and, despite its relatively small weight, this action results in a slight mechanical squeal. I groan and let myself collapse, eliciting yet another shriek from the mattress. Ana wasn't kidding.

Hey, God? Now I know I said I didn't need much, but you seriously have to be messing with me. This is the kind of thing I was so lucky to avoid at Claire's place. And she wasn't an asshole, either.

The gun that killed Adrian and Mr. Doug Smith is pointed at me. The added weight of my ass hitting the bed must have caused it to slip out of my jacket pocket. I see the wretched agent's face, the blood dripping from his mouth. And I feel the warm jolt of the gun in my hand, the muted pop-pop, the red fountain in Mr. Doug Smith's forehead.

I give my face a good slap and push the pistol back into the pocket.

●

I'm throwing up in the bathroom toilet. Finally I pull up, turn around and look past the sink into the mirror. My hair is in wretched shape and my face looks like it's in need of a shearing. I wipe at the gobs of yellow mucus lining my lips. Then I turn around and vomit again. My ribs cry out in agony as more and more of the dark mush finds its way into the white bowl. Then the tears come.

What have I done? You fucking idiot! You fucking idiot! You've fucked everything up! You're going to be dropped! You're going to be dropped, dropped, dropped!

I breathe heavily, in and out, in and out. Adrian falls. Kira hands me a glass of blood.

I shouldn't have gone back for the killer. I should have tried to help Adrian! I could have saved his life if I wasn't so caught up in taking down the assassin. Everything would still be all right for me. I wouldn't be a killer. Adrian might be alive. Kira might be in love with me.

Kira, Kira, Kira! I keep fucking thinking about Kira! That's why I felt so sick seeing Ana and Eric embracing like that. I almost...I almost had that.

She tried to turn you in, Seven. She tried to turn you in!

No! She's been programmed by the government! It's not her fault! I could have made her see my way! We could have been happy! I see her smile. I hear her roller-coaster shriek. I feel her soft skin. I smell her golden hair. I taste her strawberry lips. Oh God. Oh God!

Knocking at the door. "You all right in there, fella?" It's Eric. I just met him but I already recognize his thick, bonehead voice.

I clear my throat. "Yeah, be right out." I flush and then pull at the toilet paper, rubbing it over first my eyes and mouth, and then the toilet seat. My elbows brush against the shower curtain.

●

I meet Eric's confused gaze with a fake smile.

"I'm not going to want to go in there for a while, am I?" he welcomes.

I keep smiling. Eat shit, man.

"It's okay, dude," he continues. "Happens to the best of us."

I walk past him. "Are the results in, yet?" I ask David.

"Yes. But it doesn't make sense."

I pause. "What?"

"You're not in the database."

"—the hell?" Ana contributes. "Even Elites are in there."

"So what does that mean? He doesn't exist?" Eric asks.

"Either he was never in the system, or they took him out." David answers. "Since I can't think of a logical reason those paranoid fucks would take someone out, I'm going to go with explanation A—he's not a citizen; he's not from around here."

Ana narrows her eyes. "But he doesn't look like a foreigner."

David shrugs. Eric scratches the back of his head.

"So," I begin. "Are we still cool, or...?" I edge slowly toward the exit.

"It changes things," David says with a glimmer in his eye. "Do you know why you're not in the system?"

Just tell them.

"No..." I'm running through the forest. "But..." I'm jumping over graves. "Well..." I'm screaming into the rain.

Tell them.

14
TURMOIL

Adrian's holding himself up on the doorway. "Sorry to wake you. It's not morning yet."

"It's fine," I say wearily, pulling myself up from the shoddy bed. "What's up?"

"I'm restless," he says. "I need my fucking guitar."

Wait, this isn't right. He doesn't even have a scratch on him. "Who are you?" I protest.

Adrian laughs. "You know who I am. What, did you lose your memory again?"

"But at the rock show," I gasp. "I saw—"

"Mr. Doug Smith's assignment—ever since my father's arrest—has been to watch me. He's been waiting for me to crack. I mean, I certainly didn't think I cracked, man, but the Guard have always been better at determining that kind of thing."

"But how—"

"Can you do me a favor?" Adrian asks, pausing to kick a ball of dust. "As I said, I want my guitar. But I can't go out there. I need you to get it for me."

"Me?!"

"It's late, and we're not really that far from the hostel. It shouldn't be too difficult."

"But the Guard are after me," I stammer. "David and Ana told me to stay here."

"I'll give you a twenty."

This is ridiculous. "Dude, I—"

"Forty."

I cough. "Forty?"

"Forty," Adrian confirms.

"I just—"

"Please, dude? The hostel isn't that far away. Make a left, go like five blocks on Easton and you're at the church. You know the way from there."

"Yeah, but—"

"Here's the key," he says, tossing it. "Don't wake anyone up."

●

The windows are dark and the traffic lights blink yellow. The trees sway gently, like somebody's set the world to slow motion. A chill in the air encourages me to pull my jacket tighter against my body. It must have just rained—the street is shining like a waxed car.

I wonder what time it is, but it's too dark to read my watch— Adrian's watch.

None of this makes sense. I should have asked Adrian more questions. But come to think of it, I barely remember walking out the door. It's like I'm in the forest again, only now I've got nothing to hope for.

This is stupid. God, why did I agree to this? The Guard might know what I look like now…and anyway, won't it be suspicious being out this late?

I lose my bearings and start hyperventilating.

Oh, God…

I start running. Faster and faster.

●

I stop short at the church. The giant cathedral's stained-glass windows emit blood-red light. They look like eyes, watching me.

I move into the shadows. Something crackles behind me. I spin around, but can't find the source. Again, I run.

●

I can barely see the doorknob. I scratch at it with the key until the object finally, miraculously, slips into place. I hold my breath and turn, then gently push the door open.

The wind whooshes into the entryway. I shuffle in and push the door closed.

No light.

C'mon, eyes. Adjust, damn it!

The stairs appear. I hold my breath and take them slowly, one at a time. But the old house creaks with every step.

Adrian's door is ajar. Inside, all his shit is strewn around the floor. Someone had been in here, searching.

My eyes land on the guitar case. Apparently, the Guard didn't want it. I flip open the top to make sure it's in there, and then buckle it shut.

The stairs wail louder on the way down. The guitar isn't heavy, but a bit awkward to handle. I get it outside.

I should have asked for more cash.

"What've you got there?" a voice from the street demands. It belongs to a scraggly beggar type with a gun. He looks straight out of a comic book. "Give me it," he says.

I play the game and hand it over.

"Thanks, kid," he laughs, putting the gun back in his pocket and turning away with the instrument.

I reach into my jacket. "Stop, Heretic," I say. "That doesn't belong to you."

For a second, I let him gape at the pistol in my hands. Then I let him have it.

The first shot lands in his leg. The second shatters his right hand, and the third hits him between the eyes. He crumples onto the floor.

I stroll toward the weapon on the ground, pick it up and remove the ammunition.

•

There's a loud crash and the scene pops. My eyes open and take in a grimy ceiling. My skin is wet with sweat.

"Dammit Eric, be careful!" Ana yells outside my room.

"It's all good," her boyfriend comforts. "Sorry, babe."

Real world realities come flooding back. Last night, they asked me to join the Underground. I said I'd sleep on it, and now I had.

"Shit," I groan, attempting to sit up. The movement is futile—my back aches too much. I roll off the mattress instead. It squeaks noisily.

Stumbling into the hideout proper, I find Ana and Eric cuddling on the floor around a plastic grocery bag. No sign of David. "Oh!" she gasps, pulling fast away from her boy toy. "Sorry about the noise. Did we wake you?"

"Don't worry about it," I say. "Saved me from a nightmare."

"Adorable," says Ana.

Eric snorts.

"Well, anyway," Ana says, "I got you breakfast and some other stuff from the store."

Eric picks up the bag and tosses it at me. I snatch it out of the air and eye its contents: toaster pastries, orange juice, shaving razor and cream, toothbrush, toothpaste, 5-pack of black T-shirts, 6-pack of socks.

"If you need anything else, let me know," she chirps.

"You do remember how to use all that shit, right?" Eric asks.

"Yeah," I say. What a jerk.

I guess I should tell them that I'll join.

No, not yet. Still need to think.

I bring the bag back into my room and eat by myself. The breakfast tastes like heaven, which means it must not be very good for me. I stuff the last strawberry-filled crust into my mouth and wipe my hands on my pants. Then I snatch a few of the hygiene utensils from the bag and head for the bathroom.

•

The smell of vomit still lingers, but it's not as bad as yesterday. I take a glance at the wolf in the mirror and instinctively reach for the shaving razor. It turns out to be more of a shred, and I cut myself in the process. I move on to my teeth—brush, swish and spit. Finally I scorch my face with hot water and soap.

I pull off my shirt. I've still got the blood and sweat from the rock show all over me. What I really need is a shower.

The hot water feels like a blanket...almost makes me think I'm back in bed. But then my incessant mind starts ticking again.

Should I join them? David can't explain why I woke up in a forest without memory either, but he was quick to point out the advantages. The government can't keep track of me—I could skip church for the rest of my life and no one would care. He also seemed pretty impressed I killed an Elite Guard and got away.

I see Mr. Doug Smith's bulging eyes and twist the shower off hard.

But what's in it for me? This nation might be fucked up, but it's not my home—not really, anyway. Adrian's murder was horrible, yeah, but I got my revenge for that already, right? Right now I just need to take care of myself. I need a safe, comfortable place to stay, and I need money.

Damn it. I forgot to ask for a towel.

•

"Heeey," Ana sings over Eric's shoulder as I step out of the bathroom. She's clearly amused that I've got my shirt wrapped around my dripping waist. I smile at her and then scurry into my room.

Putting on fresh clothes again makes things feel slightly less hopeless. Ana agrees when I reemerge from my nook: "Wow, you look sharp, boy." She gazes at me bemusedly, like a cat. I look around for Eric. The awkward silence is interrupted by a flushing toilet.

Finally, I thank her. Then I find myself stammering, "You too." What was that?

Ana smiles lightly.

Eric returns and traps her against his chest with his tree-like arms, eliciting a high giggle. He looks in my direction with surprise. "Whoa, what gives, dude? You don't look like shit, anymore."

I ignore him. "So are there a lot of these hideouts?" I ask Ana.

Ana grins. "There are always more mice than the cats know."

"Don't mind her, she's just a dumb chick," says Eric.

"Hey!" laughs Ana, nuzzling against his neck.

"So when do you think David will get here?" I ask.

"After he's done work...five or so," she says with a glance at her bare wrist.

117

"Speaking of which," Eric cuts in, "we should really get going, babe."

Startled, Ana snatches Eric's wrist to take a gander at his shiny gold watch. "Shit!" She makes a mad dash for the door; her beau follows lazily. "Bye Seven, I'll be back at four."

I go back to my room to lie down. The bed squeaks.

•

A gentle guitar melody. My eyes open and it cuts out. I realize it was the tune Adrian played when he got shot, and I see Doug Smith's steely glare.

I squeeze my pillow until the killer's eyes pop. That son of a bitch! I could kill them all and Adrian would still be dead!

The rain falls hard and the forest is flooding. I run but keep falling. Now I'm swimming. I grab onto a tree branch and climb forever. I reach the top; I can see forever and the city is ablaze.

"You goddamned Heretic!" the black-eyed blonde screams up at me.

"Kira—" I whimper.

She cackles. "You can't run, Seven. There's no point. They'll find you. They always find you." She sings: "You're going to get dropped, Seven. You're going to get dropped! You're going to get dropped! You're going to get dropped, dropped, dropped!"

A giant jet-black dragonfly tears over the orange horizon. I nearly lose my grip in the wind. The helicopter's guns light up and rattle a terrible cacophony. I let go of the branches.

•

"Wakey wakey," sings Ana, shaking me alert. Her eyes are filled with something like jubilation and it reminds me of Kira. "Have you been asleep all day? Get on up, I got us all some tasty dinners from the Eat 'N Go!" She dashes away.

I get some strong déjà vu of breakfast. There again is Ana and Eric camped out on the floor, only this time they're munching on hamburgers. I join them.

Tell them you'll join.

No, not yet. I'm still not sure.

"This is so goddamned good," Ana says. A few crumbs of

processed beef slip out of her mouth. "Oh, gross. Babe, get me a napkin."

Eric takes a moment to chew, laughs, and obliges her.

"So what do you Heretics do anyway?" I ask suddenly.

"What?" Ana chokes.

"Do you take pictures? Do you write reports? What do you do here that the government wouldn't want you to be doing?"

"Well," Ana stalls. "Basically, we're journalists doing their job. If you haven't noticed, the government is pretty much shit, but everyone's too scared to expose it for what it is. We're not scared."

"You've exposed them?"

"Eventually...right now we're just collecting the dirt."

I nod and take a few bites from my burger. "So," I say with a strange hand flourish. "Does this job pay?"

Ana's eyes widen slightly. "Well, I mean..."

"It pays," Eric affirms with a munch. "Not enough to cover rent, but it pays."

I should just tell them that I'll join. I'm not getting the bookstore job back, and I need these people for protection. If I can save up some cash, maybe I can pay my way out of the country and get a fresh start. And in the meantime, serving the public good just might relieve some of the tension.

Okay, then, tell them you'll join.

"You look like you're thinking that last one over pretty damn hard, man," laughs Eric. "Any more questions to push out or you constipated?"

"Eric," Ana whines.

Tell them you'll join.

"I'm decided now," I say. "I want to help."

"Well that's a relief," Eric snickers. "I thought that vein in David's forehead was going to burst yesterday when you said you were going to think things over."

"Maybe I felt guilty."

Ana cracks up. Eric's smirk stays glued to his face. "Well, that's good news, dude, because we've got a mission tonight," he says. "I'm sure we can find something for you to do."

15
REBELS

As much as I enjoy carving out a little niche in the backseat with my ass, I'm supposed to be the getaway driver. But I don't think David is actually planning to let me drive at all. It's his car, and the man is way too protective to let someone else press its buttons. I bet he's one of those guys who waxes it every chance he gets.

Eric yawns in my ear. Ana's trying to read a map, even though the only light is coming from the street.

I wish they'd tell me where exactly we're going. "Some kind of science lab" is pretty vague. They obviously don't trust me yet.

"Make a right at the light," directs Ana.

"Are you sure?"

"David, I'm reading the map," she seethes.

"Okay, okay! Cool down, baby!" he protests, lifting his hands off the wheel. The car jerks to the left a bit and his hands come back down hard. "Seven, you gonna be all right?"

"Yeah, I'm good."

"You know what you're supposed to do?"

"Yeah."

"Tell me."

Is he serious?

"Seven?"

"I'm going to wait in the car."

"Damn straight you are!" he cheers. "And if we come runnin'?"

"I start the ignition, wait for you all to get in, and we go."

"Good man!" David says. "You can drive stick, right?"

"Yeah." At least I think so. Wish he'd let me practice with the car.

"And don't drive off nowhere, not even around the block."

"What if someone tells me to move?"

"What, like the Guard?"

"Yeah, or just some security guy or something."

"Well," David says, considering. "I guess you just drive around the block then. But don't go far! We have to be able to find you."

"Right."

"Everyone else knows what they're doing?"

Ana and Eric offer variations of yes.

●

The car slows. "We're close, right?" David asks Ana.

"Yeah, it's a couple blocks down."

"We'll park here, then." David looks over his shoulder a few times, shifts into reverse, and eases the car ever so delicately against the curb. "You'll be all right with the car, Seven?"

"Yeah, don't worry about it."

"Be good to her while I'm gone."

I pause. "Okay..."

The four doors pop open at the same time. I transfer my ass to the driver's seat. David brushes his hand against the hood of the car and whispers something. He does a cute little jog to catch up with Ana and Eric, already halfway down the block. The trio turns the corner and I'm all alone.

●

It's dark and quiet. There's nothing interesting to look at. Even if I had a book, I couldn't put the light on to read—that would call attention to the car.

What am I even doing here? Is it really a good idea to get involved with an organization like this? I just got into trouble with the Guard. I may have escaped that, but now I'm just getting myself into more shit.

And why would I help these people? They're all jerks—I don't fit in here any more than I did with the so-called Patriots. These people aren't my friends; why would I feel the need to help them? It has to be more than the money; this isn't the kind of job you do just for the money. If I wanted to get out of the country so bad I wouldn't dig myself into a deeper hole.

Maybe it's because this is what I think Adrian would have wanted. I only knew him for a few days, but he really was a friend. Maybe that's what it comes down to; I'm doing what Adrian said he was going to do. These people may be bastards, but I guess they're fighting against something pretty awful.

I just wish they would tell me what they were doing. They brought guns, cameras and handheld scanners. What have I become a part of? Who's to say these guys are any better than the Guard?

•

Gray steam billows out of a vent down the road. It curls and fades into the night sky. I wonder if the Metro is around here—and I wonder what happened to that crazy drunk I smashed my foot into?

For some reason, the memory makes me smile.

"Maybe I should go back to church," I say, falling into a hearty chuckle.

God. Anyone passing by would probably be concerned about me. They wouldn't even ask what I was doing here. They'd just right away send me to the crazy house.

•

Was Kira really going to turn me in? I didn't hang around to ask questions. I just ran. Maybe there was some other explanation. What was she saying on that phone? Did she say "The Heretic is here," or was it just "He's here"?

The first would be a pretty straight-forward turn in, I guess. "Heretic" isn't exactly a friendly label in this town. I hate her for that, for not talking to me first. But why would she? Maybe I'd have done the same thing in her position.

Shut up, Seven. It's not worth thinking about. You're not going to come up with any answers talking to yourself. You're just mad because the night was going so well. You're just mad because you got so close to third base.

Wait, no, it's not like that; I'm not like that. I don't care that we didn't—I just thought we had something, wanted to see it grow and so forth. You know, all that hokey shit everyone wants. Instead, the whole thing got cut down like a weed.

But that's all you are, Seven—a weed. You don't belong here and you'll never belong here. It's only a matter of time before the gardeners find you.

There's a gun on the passenger seat—my gun—just in case. I pick it up, run my hand over its smooth, ebony barrel, and then along the rounded silencer.

Fuck, where's my water? I twist in my seat and fumble around the back. My fingers rub against the soft carpet for an eternity until I finally locate the cold bottle. I untwist the cap and gulp another quarter down. Some of it gets on my shirt.

●

I switch on the radio.

"Swing and a miss, strike three!" booms a deep, scratchy voice—probably a cigarette smoker. An angry mob hisses and boos. "And that's a very important out number one for the Knights!"

"Wow, Silva got lucky with that one!" exclaims a second man. "I don't think he meant to throw that for a strike—not with runners on first and second!"

"That will bring up Hardy. Joe, the Hawks are running out of outs. For those of you joining late, we're in the bottom of the ninth. The visiting Knights are up by two. Silva is going for his 30th save this season, but the Hawks are trying to start a rally. Cuervo got the inning going with a single and then Silva walked McCarthy."

"And even with that out, Frank, this is not the inning Silva had in mind when he walked out onto the rubber. He's usually lights out with hitters."

"Keep in mind that he has blown two saves this year."

"Yep, and the Hawks are hoping to make that three."

"Silva looks ready to go. Here comes his first pitch," says Frank. "Big swing and a miss, strike one!"

"Hardy looked like he was swinging for the bleachers!" exclaims Joe. "He needs to cool down and focus on getting on base."

"Now the catcher Johnson is coming out to talk things over with Silva."

"Yeah, Johnson just wants to make sure Silva pays attention to Cuervo on second," says Joe. "Cuervo is third in the league in steals. He can really fly."

"The pitch!" bursts Frank. "That was a little low, ball one."

I fiddle with the volume. I'm not quite sure whether listening to this game is reducing my boredom.

"There appears to be a plastic bag floating around right field," says Frank. "Looks like Aaron has got it."

Okay, that's enough of that.

I change the station and get drilled by pop music. "Every time that I leave you," sings the processed voice, "I want to come back for more, more, more!" I'm not sure if it's a guy or a girl; it really could be either. The music reminds me of a gumball: the sweet flavor is short-lived, it doesn't satisfy my appetite, and I'm left with the taste of cardboard in my mouth. So I switch the station.

"—and the second cub is named Joey. You can see the little lions at the National Zoo starting tomorrow," sighs a feminine voice. "Meanwhile, President Drake and his family took a trip to an undisclosed beach today for a little fun in the sun—"

I switch the radio off.

•

It's been almost an hour since they left. No one said anything about how long this would take. I didn't ask, to be fair. I really should have asked. Not that it would have made much difference. I'd still be sitting here with my mind rattling away.

I turn the radio on again. "—killed an Elite two nights ago at the Red Lion. Guard found him hiding out in a motel room just outside city limits."

Wait, what?

"The murderer's name is Walt Dugan. Dugan will be dropped in about two hours. DAY News will have full coverage of the execution."

Walt? Not the Walt from the hostel?

I hear a yell. Eric is tearing fast around the corner, with David and Ana close behind. I slam the radio off.

A fourth figures emerges from the shadows—he's holding some kind of rifle.

I snap my gun off the seat, push my way out the door and fire. David, Ana and Eric stare at me in horror. The shadow falls.

"Holy shit!" exclaims David enthusiastically. "Holy shit!"

"Good fucking shot, dude," says Eric, running now. "I think you just saved us a trip to the morgue."

"Everyone in the car!" nags Ana. "There might be more of them on the way."

I head back for the driver's seat, but David pushes me out of the way. "Get in the back, Seven. This is my girl."

We rocket past the would-be killer. I get a glimpse of the body, but don't see his face.

•

I killed an Elite Guard named Doug Smith, but in two minutes, Walt Dugan will be executed for it. My tongue tastes bitter, like blood.

They've shown Walt's picture, and—I was right—it's the awkward kid from the hostel who gave everyone the slip on the way out to church. He might also be the son of that harried whiskey drinker I observed at the Blackbird Arms.

"I know what it looks like," David says, walking toward me and the TV. "But I'll tell you, Seven, you ain't off the hook yet!"

"But they think he did it, don't they?"

"No, they're not idiots," he answers. "They know this fuck is innocent, at least of that crime. But the Guard has to prove itself an effective force to the public. They have to maintain their stranglehold over the country."

"So why him, then?"

"He might be a thief, might be an unlucky stoner. But the public will think he's the killer, and more importantly, that there's no escape from the Guard," he says. "And there's another benefit, too. With someone else taking the fall, the real killer—you—just might get lulled into a false sense of security. Then you'll come out in the open, thinking everything is hunky-dory, and bam!" David's fist smacks into his palm. "They got you."

"Thanks for the reassurance."

"Killing an Elite is a very personal attack on the Guard," he continues. "You can't kill one of their own and get away with it, no matter what cards they flash at the public."

Pop! Walt falls through the floor.

"Don't worry about it too much though, kid. We'll keep you safe and sound."

"That's nice of you."

"Not really," he says. "Seems you've got talent with a gun, Seven. And I want to exploit it."

"Are you saying I won't be waiting in the car next time?"

"No one's going to be waiting in the car next time. In fact, that's the first time we've ever had anybody wait in the car. But I needed you to prove yourself. I didn't expect you to save our asses, but hey, that's definitely one way to do it."

If he had any idea how close I was to falling asleep...

David hits me in the arm. "Hey, you like fighting games?"

"What?"

David changes the channel and flicks a plastic gaming pad. "City Brawl 2" pops onto the screen. He hands me a controller. "Think you can take me?"

I shrug. "It's possible."

He laughs. "Need me to explain the controls?"

"I should be able to figure it out," I say. "You just mash buttons in these games, anyway, right?"

"Well," he considers, "I mean, there's some skill involved."

"Whatever."

I roll through a grid of pictures on a character selection screen, and select Chan, a thin, ninja-looking fellow with a sword. David picks a blond, muscle-bound giant called Bjorn. "I veel crush you!" my boss roars in perfect accent.

"Round one!" a thick video game voice exclaims. "Fight!"

As promised, the setting is a city—right in the middle of the street, in fact. I press buttons as fast as I can. My ninja is a lot faster than David's goliath, so I manage to get a lot of hits in. Both of our life bars are low when suddenly Bjorn's arms rise up and Chan get nailed with a bolt of lightning. The ninja sails backward in slow motion.

"Fuck yeah!" David cheers. "I'm taking you down in two rounds, boy."

"Yeah, yeah, we'll see about that."

"Round two!" yells the game. "Fight!"

Chan ducks and slices Bjorn's legs with the sword, knocking him over. The ninja leaps at the fallen gladiator and sinks the weapon into the muscleman's chest.

"You fucking cheap bastard!" yells David, slamming harder on his controller's buttons.

Bjorn gets up and uppercuts Chan high into the air. Then the behemoth jumps up and slams him back down. Chan recovers and tosses a ninja star, but Bjorn swats it out of the air. Then the giant grabs a garbage can.

"What?" I protest. "You can pick shit up in this thing? Why didn't you tell me?"

"I can't help it if you're an amnesiac," David taunts. The trash can cracks Chan in the face.

With a health bar close to nil, my ninja makes one final attempt: a flying kick. But Bjorn grabs him by the leg and slams him against the ground.

"Winner!" the game bursts. "Bjooooorn!"

"No!" I yell.

"Ah," David sighs, putting down his controller. "That felt good. Eric and Ana never want to play—say it's kid's stuff."

"Well, I guess they have each other to play with," I offer.

"Hell yeah they do!" David unleashes a deep, frightening laugh. "They fuck like rabbits! I should have made a rule about no inter-team dating!"

I nod. That would sure make things less awkward.

"What was really fucked up was this time we were on a stakeout. We were behind these bushes near a mansion, waiting for our target to pull in. Five minutes go by and there's no sign of him. Eric starts groaning about how long it's taking."

"Annoying."

"Yeah, so I tell him to shut the fuck up. Well, he quiets down, but next thing I know, Ana's moaning. Only this time, it didn't have nothing to do with the wait!"

I cringe. "Um..."

"Yeah! I was like... what the fuck?!" He shakes his head. "Shit, man, you know, as much as I resisted you joining, it's good to have another clear-headed guy around," he says.

"Clear-headed?" I say. "Pun intended?"

"Oh shit, that's fucked up!" he cackles, teeth bared. "Oh man, that's some pretty funny shit!"

"I try."

"But yeah man, with you around, I can at least separate them on missions. There's nothing worse than watching them cuddle-fuck on a stakeout. In fact, I'll probably do that tomorrow night."

"Watch them cuddle-fuck?"

"Ass." The grin is again horrifying. "I'm saying we have another mission tomorrow night."

"Yeah?" I say. "Do I get to know what it's about this time?"

He nods slightly. "More information gathering—same stuff we did tonight. Basically, government's building some kind of tiny video camera."

"Tiny video camera?" I repeat.

"It's scarier than I make it sound. The idea is a tiny video camera is easier to camouflage and conceal. Maybe they'll put them in homes—not sure. Point is, if these things hit the streets and we're not ready, the Guard is gonna start pullin' in a bigger net of fish."

"More people watched."

"Yeah, and more executions."

16
THE WAR AT HOME

"Daniel Alexander Young leads the Underground?" I repeat.

Ana's hand snaps to her mouth. "Oh, uh," she stammers. "Shit."

"It's okay," says David. "Seven proved himself yesterday. As far as I'm concerned, he's an official member of the team."

He turns to me. "Seven, Young is the reason the Underground exists."

"You know who he is, right?" Eric says, half-chewed pizza crust dribbling out of his mouth.

"I saw him at church," I say. Didn't recognize him at the time, of course, but that's not important. "He's rich and owns a lot of shit. He leads the Underground?"

"Of course he does. We couldn't survive without him. Young has the money, the direction. We'd be lost without him."

"Huh," I consider. "Wait, so is that what the DAY on the bank outside stands for? Daniel Alexander Young?"

"Duh," remarks Eric. "Why do you think we use a DAY cash machine as the entrance to our little hideout here?"

I force a smile.

"Wait a minute," he whines. "David, didn't you show him the orientation video yet?"

"Oh," grumbles David. "Shit, that's right." He spins his chair, pushes off the wall and slides across the floor to a table. He opens one drawer, slams it shut. He slides to a file cabinet, opens and

131

slams another drawer. "Shit," he says again.

"I'm sorry," I say. "What's this about?"

"It's like, the fucking...you know, like, the fucking orientation."

I look at Ana for explanation. She rolls her eyes.

"I'm supposed to make newbies watch it," David says, poking through a pile of cheeseburger wrappers on his desk. "In fact, technically, I'm not supposed to let anybody out on a mission without showing it to them."

Eric chuckles. "You lost it, didn't you?"

David does the smart thing and ignores the jerk. "Aha!" he bursts suddenly. A shiny disc is in his hand. "I think this it."

"Sure that's not your mountain goat porn?" Eric smirks.

"Let it go!" David exclaims, shaking his head in disgust. He waves at me. "Seven, come over here."

David directs me to sit in his computer chair and passes me a giant pair of headphones. They're ratty like everything else in this hole.

"So what's this about mountain goat porn?" I ask.

"Forget it," he says, popping the disc in the drive. He fiddles with the mouse and the screen goes black. "Okay, have fun."

●

A fire-eyed black silhouette appears on screen—the face of the Underground. A clean cut, salt-and-pepper-haired businessman strolls into view.

"Hello, my friends," the suited man says. His voice is squeaky. "My name is Daniel Alexander Young. Welcome to the Underground."

Snap to a grainy, black-and-white video of President Drake. A microphone obstructs only a portion of the man's maniacal grin. In slow motion, his eyes shift back and forth. He looks like a snake.

"Every day," says Young's voiceover, "the government tightens its grip around the necks of the citizens. Deviation is not tolerated. Dissent is punishable by death. As the old expression goes, 'Patriots are the true. Heretics are the damned.'"

Cut to a Young close-up. His eyebrows are arched. "But in its slogan, the government left out an important final point: Until the Guard proves us Patriots or Heretics, we, the people, are the Watched."

The camera zooms out. "But let's back up for a minute, for it is in the past where our fascist present is rooted. The government's largest crime has been its suppression of history. But not all of us have forgotten the true chain of events.

Cut to a bustling city street. A woman and her chipper children are buying apples and other fruit at a stand. The seller laughs jubilantly.

Young continues: "We should be free to practice whatever religion we choose—this is what creates a diverse, vibrant culture. Unfortunately, there are some who become caught up in their beliefs. They have no tolerance for any alternative."

Fade to a bunch of folks in their Sunday best, moseying into church.

"Before the war, there existed a great diversity of religions. President Frederick Wright, his government and the majority of citizens belonged to the old Church, which is the same as today's Church. But there was another temple, led by the minister Joseph Fink. And it was winning converts and growing fast."

Fade to a jolly-looking priest wearing white and gold. At the altar, he reads from a large leather-bound book.

"If Wright was a rational man, he would have seen this second Church as the miraculous result of a free, democratic nation. But Wright was not a rational man. The President did not embrace Fink's religion; he instead saw a threat to the traditions our great nation was founded upon. He had to destroy it."

Cut to a burning government building, filmed in sepia. "Wright's opportunity came on a day of great disaster—the day criminals infiltrated and laid waste to the Capitol Tower. Our shocked nation begged for answers. Wright went on the radio and gave us some."

An image of Wright and a crackly recording: "We have captured the devils! Their leader kneels before me now, handcuffed and bloody. I have asked him here so he might explain himself."

Snaps, pops and silence. "Apocalypse is coming!" a new voice shouts, apparently Joseph Fink. "Citizens, you must repent! Destroy what's old and follow Fink to glory! Kill and destroy! Pave a path to heav—"

"Enough," scolds President Wright. "Citizens, you've just heard the name of the devil—Fink—Joseph Fink ordered the bombing! Joseph Fink ordered the destruction of our great nation! We cannot and we will not have that. Fink and his flock must be dealt with."

"And then," says Young. "Wright took one step further into madness."

"This is a message to all of Fink's followers!" the crackly voice blares. "You have one week to convert to the true Church and repent for your sins! If you do not convert, we will consider your refusal a declaration of war!"

The crackling dissipates.

"That's how it began," Young says. "We do not know the identity of the man Wright interviewed, but we are certain he had no ties to Joseph Fink."

A man is led handcuffed down the street. A Guard snags a little girl by the collar, violently lifting the child into his arms.

"Wright killed Fink. Thousands of other deaths followed."

A small temple explodes. A man is held at gunpoint. Another hangs by the neck.

Close-up of a burning house. Within, a woman screams.

"Things got worse," Young says. "Wright called for a strengthening of national security."

Another image of the demon President. "Never again!" Wright crackles. "Never again will we allow Heresy to spread in our fair land. Never again will we allow attacks on our people, or our values."

Young shakes his head. "After that, Wright revealed plan after plan to, in his words, 'fortify the nation.' If we refused to submit, Wright said, we were sure to be attacked again. Out of fear, we, the people, believed him. Our fear made us the Watched."

Cut to a stark, metallic church. "Today, the Church is the heart of the paranoia machine, a forum for state propaganda. Every week, the Church holds the people captive. Every week, the Church teaches the people to hate deviation."

Back to Young.

"But the terror program stretches far beyond the steel walls of the Church. Shortly after the war, the government launched a national surveillance program called 'Hawkeye.' Under this bold intrusion of personal privacy, the government's ears spied on citizens' phone conversations and its fingers flipped through emails, library records, credit card invoices and website logs.

"At first, there was resistance. Some tried taking the Guard to court, claiming breaches of basic privacy rights. One case even made it to the highest court in the Capital.

"But the Guard successfully defended the program as an important homeland security initiative, designed to keep the nation safe from Heretic attacks. They said the program targeted only a small but dangerous portion of the overall population—members of a Watched List."

Another execution video.

"And then they found dirt on the resisters and pinned them as Heretics."

The victim drops.

Young sighs.

"Most citizens don't realize how frequently they're under the lens. The majority knows about the surveillance program, but believes the government when it says it only targets a select list of potentially dangerous individuals called the Watched.

"That belief is naïve. A Watched List exists, yes, but you don't need to be on it to be monitored. If you have any contact with a Watched—over the phone or through email are just a few examples—you are also watched. The approach is indirect, yes, but you are watched nonetheless. And if the Guard hears you saying something even slightly critical—even slightly heretical—they're liable to add you to the Watched List. We've seen it happen time and time again.

"Of course, the government would never tell you that. The

details of the surveillance program are classified—for the Guard's eyes only. They say they can't tell us about the program, because doing so…"

President Drake flashes onto the screen and completes the sentence, "…would pose a significant threat to national security."

Young winks. "But it's a bit ironic of them to claim a national surveillance program shores up national security. The truth is, spying on citizens does not protect a nation against attack—it tightens the government's control of only its own people. No, surveillance has never been about protecting the country. 'Protecting the country' is just an excuse to violate private liberty; a means to a single, paranoid end."

Young's eyes are fixed, methodical. "Soon, we will all pay the price for being so near-sighted."

A dusty battleground. A squad of soldiers lying out on the sand takes shots at an unseen Enemy.

"Today, we are engaged in another, separate war overseas. But we cannot win there—not when the government is so focused on so-called Heretics within our borders."

Black jets soar through blood red skies.

"The truth is, we've not fortified our nation at all. There is nothing to stop the Enemy from attacking the homeland.

"If the war ever came home—if the Enemy ever found a way to attack us directly—what will it matter if someone skips church? What will it matter if someone condemns the government for what it is?"

Young smiles warmly. "Change is coming. I formed the Underground to expose and topple the government that oppresses us.

"President Drake and the Guard hold the homeland hostage. The government has destroyed three of our founding father's greatest ideals: peace, liberty and justice! But we still have hope. Oh yes my friends, we still have hope!

"The people are not happy. They may not yet know how to create change, but they do wait for it. My brother, we are the change. And one day soon we will ignite the people into revolution!

"The Underground grows in size every day. We are thousands, tucked away in holes, corners and shadows throughout our fair nation."

A blood-red map pulses.

"We have factions in every major city, collecting intelligence that will be used to gain the support of the people and provide insights into the Guard's weaknesses."

Young's blue eyes expand across the screen.

"Do you see, my friends? We will convince the people that we are the right.

"But take heed! The citizens have been conditioned their entire lives to side with the Guard. It is imperative we tread carefully. After all, we cannot have a revolution without the people on our side."

A man and a woman wearing masks sneak through the shadows of a warehouse. The woman stops and holds up a hand.

"As an Underground operative, it's your job to gather information and find weak points in the oppressors' armor. Your team leader will supply you with carefully orchestrated missions. For your own safety and privacy, it is imperative that you follow his or her instructions at all times."

Young straightens his tie. "Remember: we may be the Watched, but we don't have to be seen."

An array of guns and knives.

"Force will sometimes be required to complete your missions, and we will supply your team with weapons appropriate to the objectives. However, it is important to remember that our priority is to collect information. Use of guns, knives and other weapons should be limited strictly to protection. This is for both you and your team's safety."

Young holds up a finger.

"There is another important aspect of your job. The reason we have had such success, the reason we have lasted this long is because of people like you. I urge you to spread our message of revolution to family and friends, and I urge you to encourage all who are capable to come join us!"

The camera zooms in on Young's cool eyes.

"It won't be difficult. Simply reveal to them how they've been conditioned. Reveal to them the extent of the government's control! Reveal to them that the Underground means change!"

The camera zooms out.

"Now, go forward, my friends! Bring change to the people!"

17
MASKS

My shoulders tense up—we're getting close to the factory. It's going to be my first real mission with the Underground, and if David has his facts right, it's not going to be a cake walk.

What we learn tonight could set the citizens over the edge. If we find what David thinks we'll find, we might have the kind of shit that starts a revolution.

I snap a scope onto my gun.

"Don't worry," Ana purrs. "Security will be light. They'll never know we were there."

"Right," I mutter. "Because I guess they wouldn't have any kind of advanced surveillance there."

"Okay, they might see us," shrugs Ana. "But we'll be wearing these." She hands Eric and me black nylon.

"Socks?" I ask.

"Masks."

"Well, thank God for that," Eric says. He resumes his vacant stare out the window.

There are still a few things I don't get. It's easy to say you're going to start a revolution, but the logistics are mind boggling. How exactly do you tell citizens that the government can't be trusted? Even if you had a way to get the message out, why would the average citizen believe an organization of so-called Heretics?

No, Young knows what he's doing. He must have it all planned out.

"Eric, are you all right?" David says, peering through the overhead mirror.

Ana's boy toy turns away from the window and rasps, "Yeah I'm good. Just get a little jittery before missions, sometimes."

"Relax, baby," coos Ana, patting his leg with her free hand. I want to throw up. It's bad enough they touch each other so much. But I absolutely can't stand it when they talk like toddlers.

The ocean comes into view, pulling my thoughts back to Kira, my blond femme fatale. You could call her that, right? I don't know, it sounds good. What would I do, exactly, if I saw her again?

•

"Put your mask on," says David. Our faces disappear.

Gravel pops and scrapes beneath the vehicle. The noise fades into a distant mechanical humming. Following the others' lead, I push gently on my door and step out into the bleak industrial night.

The two-and-a-half story brick factory is surrounded on all sides by a large metal fence, iced with barbed wire. As feared, the cameras are everywhere, whirring left to right, right to left. Fortunately, the mission is well planned. David has found a blind spot in the factory's outdoor surveillance.

Eric cuts the fence open in the determined location, and one by one we slide through. I look through my scope and do a quick spin to make sure we're alone.

David holds his hand up. We freeze. He drops it. We dash for the ventilation duct. Eric unravels the screws, pulls it open.

The tunnel stinks. Soon I find out why: it leads into an equally smelly bathroom. In this bright room of white tile, it's obvious someone has forgotten to flush the toilet. A plop later and I realize the perpetrator is still at work.

Ana gags softly. David places an index finger over where his lips should be. He scuttles to the door and presses an ear against it. He releases his head and pushes.

Again, David holds up a hand and everyone freezes. He slips out into a hallway.

The man in the stall starts slapping his hand against the toilet paper roll, ripping and rubbing.

Isn't a little late for him to still be here? Oh, maybe it's because he's a security guard. Idiot, it's the reason you're carrying a gun.

The restroom door slides back. It's David, and now he's got blue spray paint on one of his gloves. He's disabled a camera or two. We file out of the restroom and breathe fresh recycled air. Back inside, a stall door clicks open.

We move quickly and quietly down the hallway. We stop at a T-shaped intersection, and I take in an autographed photo of President Drake on the back wall. David leans slightly into the new passage to check for anyone coming. He makes an okay sign with azure-tinged fingers, and we take a left toward some elevators and a set of fire stairs. As we turn, the heavy restroom door creaks open.

We dash for the stairs, swing open the door and begin to ascend. I look back. Through the fire exit's small glass window I see the finger of a man activate the elevator.

I wonder if he took the time to wash his hands.

•

We go up about fifteen steps, make a turn and climb fifteen more. A door on the next landing up cracks open and we all freeze. Footsteps—David leans against the railing and takes aim. The side of a man's leg appears—David fires into his ankle. The man yelps and tumbles down. I shift to the side and watch him slide past.

He's lucky; if David hadn't taken the shot, I would have targeted his forehead.

Ana's eyes flash cold at me. She jumps down the steps after the falling body.

"What?" I protest in a whisper. "Was I supposed to catch him?"

She grabs the guy by the collar, gags his mouth with a piece of cloth and handcuffs him to the railing. "We're going to have to be even quicker now," she says. "They won't find him right away, but this won't go unnoticed forever."

No one responds. We just press on.

•

David motions for us to split, and then he and Eric continue up the stairs. Our leader's made good on his plan to divide the lovebirds:

Ana and I are to observe the warehouse from this floor, the mezzanine level. David and Eric will download documents from the office.

Ana creeps along the wall to the fire door. I stand back and aim my weapon through the window. Coast looks clear, so I nod and she pulls the door open. I dash through; she follows.

I like her better when she's away from Eric. She's sharper, more rational…hell, she even looks better.

The suspended steel mezzanine cuts across the square warehouse like a giant plus sign. There's not much to it; David said it's just used as a viewing area for managers, government guests and—apparently—spies like us.

There isn't a single light on below. The workers have called it a day. The mezzanine level is dimly lit, and there are shadows everywhere—perfect for hiding. Ana snaps pictures of the boxes, conveyor belts and cutting tools below. Eventually, we come across a crate of something that seems to really excite the girl. Snap! Snap! Snap!

"What's that?" I whisper.

Ana declines to respond. Snap! Snap! Snap!

I begin to spin in a slow circle, looking for targets with my gun. Snap! Snap! Snap!

"Hey! Who's there?" a voice yells at six 'o clock. I turn hard and catch sight of a security guard. He's reaching for his rifle.

I fire a perfect shot into his neck and he shuts up.

"God, Seven," whispers Ana before turning back to her work.

•

Our partners are waiting for us back on the fire stairs. "Got 'em?" David whispers.

Ana nods.

"We found a whole lot of shit upstairs," Eric laughs. David smacks him in the head and places a finger over his mask where his mouth would be.

An alarm goes off.

"Fuck!" David exclaims.

We run down the stairs. The wounded man is gone, handcuffs

and all. But tearing upwards is another security guard. I fire, hit him in the head. He rolls comically.

"Damn!" laughs Eric. "What a shot, this guy!"

Through the exit door's tiny glass window, we notice several more meaningless guards, all grouped together by the elevators. I raise my gun again but Ana pushes it down. "There's too many of them," she justifies.

"Naw," David spits back. "There are four of 'em—one for each of us. Number them one to four, left to right. I got number one, Ana two, Seven three, Eric four."

We take aim.

"On three," our leader announces. "One, two, three!" We all fire through the glass and into the guards' respective heads. I take a second shot to finish the job.

"Now that's what I call teamwork!" David squawks.

We push through the door one by one. I almost trip over one of the corpses but catch myself.

Ana giggles. "Watch it, pal," she laughs.

I smile at the crack on the wall where one of the bullets missed target.

•

Back at the hole within the DAY bank, David slides his fourth piece of pizza down like it was an extension of his tongue. Then he grabs the camera from Ana.

"God, David, wash your hands at least."

Ignoring her, he shoves the device's memory card into the computer.

"So we're heading up the fire stairs right?" Eric jabbers on. "There's this security guard standing on the other side of the door at the top. We can literally see the back of his head through the glass of the door, right?"

"Right," Ana says after it becomes clear he won't go on without affirmation.

"So you know what David does? He fires through the glass and nails the dude! Only problem is, the guy doesn't fly forward like you'd expect; he just slides down the door! So I pull it open and the guy flops onto David's feet! David practically falls over backward!"

Ana smiles weakly.

"It was awesome," he insists. "Anyway, the office was pretty much deserted. Well, except there was this guy cursing at a copy machine in a little side area. But we were able to just sneak by, right?"

"What happened to him?" I ask.

"I dunno, I think he must have left, 'cause he wasn't there on the way back."

"Lucky fellow," says Ana.

Yeah, and he was probably the one who set off the alarm.

He looks at me. "This is so much fun, yeah?"

"What, taking pictures and killing bad guys?" I say. Can you really call that fun? "I guess it's not bad."

"That was the most action I've ever seen on a mission! I've never felt so pumped!" He whips out a pair of finger guns and points past me. "Bang, bang!"

I smile weakly. What does Ana see in this guy?

"But anyway," continues Eric, "David finds the main office, and we head in. He gets on the computer and hacks into it in like seconds. You have to see that guy hack! It's nuts! I'm guarding the door, and before I know it, David's got everything he needs on a disk! And just like that, we're out, meeting up with you guys! What took you guys so long, anyway? We were waiting for like five minutes!"

"Ana went snap-happy with the camera," I smile.

"Hey!" she protests, jabbing me lightly with her elbow. "I got a lot of good pictures!"

"So there weren't any problems?" Eric prods.

"Nope," I say. "Piece of cake."

"Well," says Ana, looking at me. "There was one little snag, but Seven took care of it."

I get an image of the security guard's neck exploding crimson.

"That was hardcore when we shot down those four guards at the end, wasn't it?" Eric starts in again.

It's like he thinks he was playing a video game. Except David said he doesn't like games—calls them kid's stuff. I guess, for him, real life is more of a thrill.

He laughs. "I was so worried I was gonna miss!"

"You did." I make guns with my fingers. "Bang, bang!"

Ana laughs. Eric's face reddens.

Now I'm sounding cocky. I've ended how many lives, now? After Mr. Doug Smith, there was the sniper outside the car. Tonight, I shot three more. That's five, and the only parts of their stories I know are the endings. And yet, I don't really feel much remorse. I only feel guilty that I don't feel guilty. But then, what I did wasn't anything personal; I did it for the greater good, right? They killed Adrian, and they'll kill hundreds, maybe thousands more like him. It's not like I'm just killing for the hell of it.

"HQ is gonna love this shit!" David exclaims from the computer. "Seven…real nice job considering you're a newbie."

Ana's hand is on my shoulder. "Yes, very well done."

I gnaw on my pizza crust. "Is it enough?" I ask.

Ana brushes aside the stupidity of my question and answers matter-of-fact: "That's up to HQ."

"Well," says Eric, standing up. "I think I'm gonna head out. Sleepy."

No one responds.

"You coming, Ana? David?"

"Naw," David answers. "You head out without me. I want to see how much respect we get from HQ for this shit. Hah!"

"I think," starts Ana, "I think I might hang out a little longer, too." She's eying me like a cat.

"Suit yourself." Eric grabs a jacket and moves for the door. Ana joins David at the computer, leaving me sitting on the floor alone.

Suddenly, David is swearing. "Fucking slow Internet!"

I stand up and move for my own quarters.

●

I shut my door and collapse on the bed. The springs scream.

What a shitty bed. If only Claire's hostel was still an option.

A knock and the door cracks open.

"Seven?" It's Ana. "May I come in?"

I sit up on the edge of my bed. "Yeah."

She walks in and takes a seat beside me. The bed squeaks. "I'm sorry you have to sleep on such an awful bed."

"It's fine."

"Know what sucks?"

"What?"

"Church is in two days."

I laugh. "I guess I don't have to go anymore, considering I don't exist."

"I know, you bastard!" she says with a beguiling smile.

She gazes at her feet.

"May I ask you something?" she says at last.

"Shoot."

"Are you," she pauses. "Are you okay with the job?"

"What?"

"I mean, you know, the violence. You don't have a memory. You don't remember the corruption and the suffering like the rest of us do. You might think you've got a pretty good motivation for helping out, but I worry if it's strong enough to keep you sane."

"Is there something wrong with what I've been—?"

"No, you've been great. Really great, actually. I just want to make sure you're okay." Ana looks into me.

"I'm okay." I shiver slightly. "Thanks for the concern, I guess."

"Do you hate it here? I mean, this nation?"

She's not going to let this go, is she? "Um," I start.

"It's horrible, I know, but you have to remember there are just as many friends living here as there are enemies. If there weren't, we might as well leave and start over somewhere else. But we stay and we fight because this is a country worth saving."

"I don't have many friends."

"Hey," Ana smiles brilliantly. "I'm your friend."

I don't say anything to that. I almost want to kiss her, but I don't do that either. I want Kira.

"Listen Seven, I'm going out to a club tomorrow night with a few friends," she says, "and you're coming with us."

"Is that an order?"

"It's a strong recommendation."

"Are Eric and David going?"

"David, no, but Eric might meet us."

I hesitate. "Is there cover?"

"Goddammit, Seven, you're going," she beams. "If you don't have the money, I'll pay your way in."

I grumble and acquiesce.

"That's better." The springs squeak as Ana pushes herself off. "Well, looks like my work here is done. Have pleasant dreams, Seven."

Pleasant dreams. Yeah, right. This night club better not suck. The last time I went out for entertainment, my friend got shot in the head.

I shouldn't let Ana pay. I don't want to look like a cheap bastard.

Oh shut the fuck up, Seven. You're poor. You can accept a little charity.

Wait, wait, I should be getting some cash from the job tonight, shouldn't I? Fuck yes! I bet this one will pay more, too, given how much more involved I was in the action.

Yeah, but aren't you saving the money to get out of the country, moron?

Oh, yeah, right. God damn it. This cover better not be expensive. Oh God, and I'm going to have to buy drinks, aren't I? This is a really bad idea, isn't it?

Well, it might be fun. You might meet some hot babe.

No, I just want to see Kira again. And what's Ana's deal? What does she really think about me? And how close is she actually to Eric? They must be pretty damn close. They're always smooching, aren't they? David's sick of it, they're so attached.

I hate them the most when I'm trying to read or something and I look up and they're cleaning each other's teeth. I can't stand them. I hate living here. I hate this goddamned country. I need to get the hell out of here, get somewhere safe—somewhere I can just start my life over again and not have to worry about survival so much.

Should I ask David about getting paid? He's still out there. Maybe I should ask.

No, that would be awkward. I mean, he might get the idea I'm only doing this for the money—which I'm not. I believe in the Underground. They're going to bring change to this oppressed country.

Maybe if I brought it up real carefully? I know, I'll go out there and ask him if HQ said anything, and then he'll get all giddy and stuff, and then I'll bring up the money situation, and, um, yeah. We'll go from there.

•

David's still sitting at the computer when I manage a reentry.

"Hey," I say.

"Ana didn't stay very long after Eric left," he meditates. "I wonder if they're having issues again."

"They seemed fine to me earlier."

"That's 'cause couples have their own language," says David. "They silent fight. Seem happy one minute, and then bam! Break up. It's fucked up."

"You think they're going to break up?"

"I hope not!" he hoots. "They make me sick, yeah, but I can't afford to lose either one of them to another team just 'cause they refuse to see each other!"

"Right, right," I say. "So, get a response from HQ?"

"Yeah, man," he says. "It's just like I said. This stuff is the shit. They're eating it up like it was filet fucking mignon."

"Cool," I say. "So, um," I pause.

"What's on your mind?"

"Does that mean we get more money for this one?"

David turns from the computer and looks at me like I was a lengthy receipt from the grocery store. Suddenly, a grin pops onto his face. "Hell yes we are!"

"Awesome," I return the smile. "So, when do you think—?"

"Chill, man! What, do you have a loan shark after you or something?"

"No, I was just wondering—"

"Probably in a day or two. HQ has got to wire it over."

"Right, that makes sense."

"Damn straight. Now why don't you get some sleep, killer? You've got to be tired after everything tonight."

"I think I will," I say slowly. "Wait, what'd you call me?"

He shrugs. "Take it as a compliment."

18
SWEAT

If the light didn't cast such a neon blue glow on everything, you might think it was day. This may be, second only to perhaps the church, the most fake and gaudy place in the city. But the people in this line don't seem to care. Everyone seems to be wearing his or her sluttiest outfit. Even the guys are wearing makeup.

I don't think this is my scene.

"This club Lauren and I went to last night was amazing!" Ana's friend Tom exclaims. "You and Nikki should have been there!"

"Eh," Lauren shrugs. "It was okay. Tom just got a high from all his tongue-wrestling."

Tom giggles. "Well, yes, I suppose I may have been wearing my rose-colored glasses last night."

The brick building is labeled *Candy* in big pink letters. A faint pulse emanates from within. The rhythm is regular, thick and mocking. It seems to taunt: "Hey, guess what suckers? People are having fun in here!"

"Well as long as you didn't find your wrestling opponent wearing them," says Ana.

"Now, Ana, you know I have standards."

"The guy was actually kinda hot," says Lauren. "I woulda done him."

"You mean if it weren't for…?" says Nikki.

"Hey, I dunno," she retorts. "Maybe he swings for both teams."

"You should have asked," Nikki smirks. "You could have had a threesome."

"I don't share," deadpans Tom. He flashes his tongue.

I look away.

•

This has seriously got to be the slowest line I've been on in a long time. Wait, I guess I wouldn't remember, would I? But I mean, come on, we moved faster than this through the traffic jam on the way over!

"What time does cover go up again?" I ask.

"In a half hour, darling," answers Tom. "We have plenty of time."

I half-smile and then resume my neck-straining stare off to the side.

"So you're sure this place is going to be good?" Nikki whines.

"Nikki, like, chill," moans Lauren. "My sister was here last week. She said it was amazing."

"And she didn't black out that night? Because she does that a lot if I recall."

Lauren's jaw drops. "What?!"

"All I'm saying is that girl must thank God every day for birth control."

"What?!"

"Nikki," whines Ana.

"I'm sorry," she says. "I just wanna get in there."

And I just wanna get this night over with. Why did I even agree to come here? This was a stupid idea. These people aren't my friends. And I need to be saving my money! How the hell am I going to get out of this country if I keep throwing my money away?

"—right, Seven?" Ana suddenly asks.

"What? Yeah I'm fine."

"No," Ana sings. "I was just saying how excited I am about this new club, and that I know we're all going to have a great time!"

"Oh."

"And then, I said, 'Right, Seven?'"

"Oh, I see."

The response doesn't shake her stare. "I mean... right."

"All right then," she concludes. Case closed.

Tom chuckles. He just caught me gazing at Lauren's balloon-like breasts. To call the blonde's red dress "low-cut" would be like calling the universe "pretty big." Nikki is a bit more conservative but her face is made up like a clown. Ana's cheeks are redder and more apple-like than I remember. They all look like plastic flowers.

"Does my hair look all right?" Tom asks Lauren.

"It looks beautiful," she says, "Spiky, yet somehow fluffy; just the way I like it."

"Wait," says Nikki. "How do you like it?"

Ana glares at her.

"You know," Lauren bubbles on. "So there's a little bounce, but not too much."

"Not too much bounce, huh?"

"Yeah," she says. "A lot of bounce is like, trying too hard, you know?"

"And I'm sure that's very exhausting for you."

"Yeah," she says. "Wait, what?"

•

A burly man in a headset approaches. "IDs?"

"Um," I stutter as Tom hands his card over. I still don't have an identity, let alone an ID card!

Ana looks at me. "Oh," she turns to the bouncer. "My friend here left his at home," she says.

"Can't let him in," the giant says.

Lauren presses against him. "Please? He's cool. It won't happen again."

He chuckles slightly. "Well..."

"Please?" Ana chimes in.

The troll steps aside. "Pay the man at the door."

"Thank you!" oozes Ana.

I reach into my pocket and pull out a few bills. If I was a cartoon character, there'd probably be an image over my head of a flushing toilet.

"It's ironic. They let the girls pay less so the men can have more options on the dance floor," Tom explains to me.

"Right," I say. "Why is that ironic?"

"Because," Tom winks. "I'm here for the boys, too."

I force a smile and then gaze at my watch. I wonder when this place closes.

Candy's beating heart grows louder until it's all I can hear. The place is dark, but there's a lot of pink and blue florescent lighting. The dance floor is packed like a can of still-alive sardines, shifting and sliding over each other.

"The bar's over there!" yells Lauren like she just saved the day. We push our way through the crowd. I say "excuse me" about eight times and then drop the phrase from my vocabulary altogether. No one can hear me, anyway.

A spritz of cold liquid splashes my neck. It smells like cheap beer. I take a deep breath and my lungs fill with smoke.

We're stopped, but the bar is close and there are too many people plastered against my back to turn around. I try to squeeze my way through. A 20-something guy wearing a pink, popped-collar polo shirt does a 180-degree turn and nearly splashes me with his beer, which apparently comes in oversized urine sample cups. What would be the results of that sobriety test?

"You," says the bartender, indicating me.

"Um, how about a rum and cola?"

The bartender fills an empty piss container with ice, drops a shot of clear unlabeled fluid and shoots some bubbly brown out of a hose. "Nine."

You have got to be fucking kidding me. Looks like this will be my only drink tonight.

I wait for the others to get their stuff and then we head out onto the dance floor. I attempt to sway back and forth to the beat. How retarded do I look right now? Does anyone notice? Does anyone care?

I take a sip. The swaying gets somewhat easier.

Some idiot pushes past me and doesn't even excuse himself.

Tom cackles like a hyena. He points off to the side at Lauren, who appears to be sucking fluid out of a man's mouth.

"That was fast," I offer.

"I love that girl!" bursts Tom.

"Oh my God!" giggles Ana. "You better catch up, Tom,"

"For real!" he exclaims. "Seven, shall we?"

"Who's doing what now?" I offer.

Ana and Nikki burst out in laughter.

"Oh my, look at his face!" oozes Tom. "The horror! The horror!"

I force a smile.

"Don't worry!" Ana says. "He doesn't bite... outside the bedroom!"

I lift a finger. "Which way is the restroom?"

I almost bowl over a short blonde.

●

The bathroom is an oasis of reggae and graffiti. I push into the only open stall and find brown liquid dripping from the toilet seat. The solitude is nice, but the smell is horrific.

I hate this place. I shouldn't have come here. You stupid fucking idiot, Seven.

"Dude, that bitch is asking for it!" someone shouts.

"Let me piss, will you?" says another.

"All I'm saying is you need to hit that shit up! I mean, c'mon, when's the last time you even saw your girlfriend? It's just fornication, man."

I open the door and move for the sinks. Suddenly, I'm being handed towels by a guy in a white dress shirt. He's got a tip coaster and some lollypops. I search my pockets and drop a penny into the dish.

●

I ascend the stairs back to the dance floor as slowly as humanly possible. Some awful song is on. The rapper alternates between the exclamations "Push it in!" and "Pull it out!"

I think about retreating.

Across the way, I see a blonde in a red dress.

Kira?

I push through the crowd. Oh my God, what am I going to say?

It's not her. For fuck's sake, Seven.

"Seven!" A hand lands on my shoulder with a jolt.

I spin around and take in Eric. He's got a pink-striped polo shirt on. The collar is popped.

"Hi," I manage.

"This place looks pretty fucking sweet."

"It's not bad," I lie.

"Where are the ladies?"

I point vaguely into the throng. "Over there, somewhere."

"Lead me, sir."

We push our way through the throng. I get more beer spilled on me.

"Oh my God, Seven, you found Eric!" bursts Ana. Ana runs at him and gives him a good squeeze. Nikki smiles. Tom is nowhere to be found.

"Let's dance, babe," says Ana.

They wander off to tangle limbs. That leaves me with Nikki. She sways a bit. I sway a bit.

"So what do you do?" I ask.

"Not very much," she says.

She sways a bit. I sway a bit.

"Hey there, hot stuff," greets some short, slimy, glasses-wearing geek.

"Oh, hi Joe."

"Dance with me, my sexy mama?"

Bewilderingly, they dance.

I sway a bit by myself. I glance to the left. Ana's grinding her ass into Eric's crotch. I look straight ahead. Lauren's hand has disappeared inside her ugly dancing partner's pants and he's grinning maniacally. I turn to the right. Casanova's head rests somewhere in between Nikki's breasts.

I can't handle this. I'm getting out.

But shouldn't I try to make the most of the cover fee?

Fuck the goddamned cover fee, it's worth more to get some fresh air and some sleep. I'm getting out of here right now.

I nearly collide with some other sucker just making his way in.

I push through the doors and fly out into the night. The air is cool against my beer-soaked skin.

I run until I find a Metro station.

19
OXYGEN

The damn thing is probably too small to do me any real harm, but reflexes don't listen to reason. My body braces for the worst. He jumps at me. The creature's big, furry paws are on my knee, and he licks my hand when I try to nudge him away.

"Romeo! Down!" barks a woman, the dog's owner. "Don't worry," she begs. "He doesn't bite. I'm so sorry."

"It's okay," I grunt.

Last night was a nightmare. I got so depressed at that club; it made me hate the entire human race. Everyone and everything was so fake, so artificial.

I think I might hate Ana and Eric. Eric is just a jerk, and Ana is just so goddamned patronizing. It's like she thinks she's better than me just because she's got her memory. She's convinced that she's got everything and that I've got nothing. That I need her pity or some shit. I don't need anything from that…that…

I suddenly get this image of her in a bed, naked and moaning heavily. The face changes to Kira.

Stop! I shake my head like a dog trying to rid itself of excess water.

A squirrel jumps out in front of me and gives me a look. Screeching car brakes from the nearest city street end the staring contest—the little guy scurries up a tree. I stroll on.

A great statue reveals itself: a man, a knight on horseback. The animal's front legs flail frozen in the air. He holds a hand to his head, looks over the trees and into the sky. He's far away from this world—it almost makes me jealous.

●

I come to a pond. Toy boats—red, green, pink and orange—bob and weave through the water. Along the edges are children holding little black boxes with silver antennas. I take a seat at one of the white benches and watch.

I wish Kira was here. I gaze to my side and try to picture what she'd look like sitting there. I see her smiling. I feel her hand on my leg.

My eyes close—and I see Kira running. The leaves are everywhere, brown, yellow and red. Her soft black jacket disappears behind the tree. I run for it and trap the girl against the oak.

"You were supposed to count," she whispers.

Her hair is soft in my hand—softer than it looked. "I love you," I say.

Her fingernail runs down my chest and I shiver.

"Excuse me," breaches the voice of some lady. My eyes open. She's middle-aged and dressed in a conservative black business suit with gray pinstripes. She's also got a toothy smile, more befitting of a shark or piranha than a human being. "Do you mind if I sit here?" Her voice slithers like a snake. "My son is playing with his boat, and well, I just can't stand for so long."

"That's fine," I say, resuming my stare at the strangely comforting boats.

A boy runs up. "There you are, mom! Where did you go?"

"I'm sorry, Dash," answers the shark woman. "Mommy got tired. You can keep playing."

"Who are you?" Dash asks me. The kid looks about six. Eight max.

"Dash!" she bursts. "Leave the gentleman alone."

I shake her off. "I'm Seven."

"That's a stupid name," says Dash.

"Dash!" mama shark protests.

"Sorry to disappoint," I answer.

The little minnow shrugs. Then he hands me his black box. "Want to try?"

"Dash!" she exclaims again. Bending in my direction, "Sir, I'm so sorry."

"Actually," I tell her. "I was a little curious. Do you mind if I...?"

"Oh by all means, go for it," she says. "I'm Joan, and this is my son, Dash." She squints her eyes at the boy. "Seven is a very nice name," she scolds.

I take the device. "Which one is your boat, Dash?"

"The blue one over there with the Spy Boy sticker."

I spot it. It's a futuristic miniature speed boat. I play with the knobs and it starts whirring into motion. It spins, zooms forward and swings back around.

"Give it back," commands Dash.

I give the boat one last sprint for the shore and then follow orders. Dash grabs it and runs away, making some kind of engine sound with his mouth.

"I'm sorry he's so rude," says Joan.

"Eh," I shrug it off. "He's a kid."

"Yes, and he has a lot to learn about the world, still," she says. "You know he only just learned his first hymn at church today."

Church. Everyone with an identity went to church today. Hard to believe that it's been a week since I was sitting in that dark cave. Claire must have gone by herself this week. After Adrian died, I never went back. I wonder if she believes the media when they say her grandson is a Heretic. She might not even know that he's dead. Maybe she thinks he's gone into hiding and that one day he will return. But how could she explain my disappearance? Was I just skipping out on the bill? Did she assume I was involved?

God, I hope Claire doesn't think I had something to do with it. Adrian was the only friend I really had in this place. He understood my situation and didn't care how I felt about the world. I wish he was still here to talk to. I hate this goddamned country so much.

Even David, Ana and Eric went to church today. They might be rebels, but it's not like that gives them a choice in the matter. They could get accused of Heresy if they don't go. It's ironic, but that could jeopardize the entire Underground.

But damn, it just seems so masochistic to do something every week you're radically against. If I ever had to go back, I don't think I could take it. Getting out of church almost makes me glad I don't have an identity.

I take in the blue sky in one deep breath. Places like this are my church.

"I swear, this boy never gets tired," says Joan. Dash completes what must be like his twentieth lap around the bench. I take a last look at the boats and then rise to my feet.

"Well, I should be going," I say. "Good meeting you."

"You too, Seven. Have a good afternoon."

"Bye, Dash," I call out.

Dash waves, keeps running.

I rise and turn home—back to the hole.

Shame I have to leave all this. So glad I got off my ass and came out here today—it's been so refreshing. I got so drained last night; I just wanted to get out. Nothing seemed worth living for. Watching all those fools drink and kiss—it was like I was in some kind of Hell. I felt worthless. And then I thought I saw Kira, and I practically knocked people over trying to get to her. I was such a desperate idiot.

God, if Adrian hadn't been shot, I'd have settled into this place in style. I had a home, a decent job, a friend and a girl. Now I've got nothing. What if there's not a mission tonight? I'm going to end up sitting in that florescent shithole all night watching the television, or maybe the bugs on the wall if they prove more interesting.

"If Adrian didn't get shot?" I repeat aloud. "What kind of fucking bullshit is that, Seven? Shut the fuck up and deal."

I just wish I could stay and watch the boats longer. I wish I was that little kid, Dash, running around benches and playing with toys.

The big rust-colored park gates amble by—I cross the street when the traffic slows. Soon I'm in front of the DAY bank, secret front for the Underground.

Someone's using the ATM.

I wait.

And I wait.

"All yours!" says the pudgy doofus, clutching a wallet almost as thick as his head.

The ATM door slams shut behind me. I slide my card with a sigh and place my hand on the scanner. The machine slides into the ceiling. "Home sweet home," I sigh.

●

"Seven, where in Hell were you?" David welcomes. He's sitting with his back to the computer for a change. Ana and Eric are gathered around him, but they spin around like a couple of tops to get a glimpse of the new arrival.

"I needed to take a walk, clear my head."

"Clear your head?" David laughs. "I thought you told me it was clear already."

"It needed some maintenance."

"Well, I hope it's fucking maintained, man. We've got a mission."

"Tonight?"

"Yeah, and it's big, so get over here and pay fucking attention."

I don't lose his angry stare until I'm firmly in my place next to Eric.

"Now as I was saying..." says David. "This," he points to an ugly mug on the computer screen, "is James T. Farnsworth."

I get a shiver. The name is somehow familiar.

"This fat fuck is a judge. He's dropped enough so-called traitors to fill a cemetery. He's killed our friends, and he's killed our family."

Oh my God—he's the one who dropped Adrian's dad! That's where I heard his name before. He's the reason Adrian's dad was murdered, the reason Adrian's mom overdosed on drugs, the reason Adrian was added to the Watched List and the reason Adrian is dead.

"Now," David says, "the judge loves baseball. Furthermore, he loves the Hawks."

"Then I guess he's not all bad," laughs Eric—the idiot.

Ana jabs him with a pen.

"The reason I bring any of this up," says David, pausing yet again to gather his excitement, "is that we just received word that the fucker will be at the baseball game tonight!"

"Are we going to give him his sentence?" asks Eric.

"We're gonna be the ones who carry it out."

"Sounds great, but—" says Ana with a pause. "I don't think Seven should go."

"What?" I gasp.

"He can't possibly understand who this guy is, what any of this means. He's not going to have the motivation, and there's no room for cold feet."

"Wait, when have I ever had cold feet?" I spit back.

"I'm just saying that—"

"I know what you're saying!" I scream. "And no, you don't have to worry about motivation on this one. I do know who this guy is! One of his sentences led to the death of my only friend in this entire fucking world—and that includes you, by the way."

Ana looks like she's about to cry. "Seven, I didn't mean to—"

"I don't just want to see him pay. I want to be the one who makes him pay."

•

Eric's at my door. "Seven, I need to talk to you."

"Okay?"

He exhales and looks down at the floor for a while. "What's your fucking problem, dude?"

"What?"

"Ana's upset."

You have to be kidding me. "What, because of before?"

"Yeah, and also last night," he says. "She's been trying really hard to make you feel welcome and comfortable here, but all you seem to do is resent her for it."

"I'll apologize to her about snapping," I say. "I felt patronized."

"She's just looking out for you, dude!" he exclaims. "And what was your deal last night? We looked all around for you and you were just fucking gone! You didn't say a word to any of us!"

"You were all occupied," I say, "and the place...it just wasn't my scene. I wasn't in a good mood, and—"

"What, do you think you're above everyone else just because of your condition?"

"My *condition*? What the fuck is that supposed to mean?"

"You think you're better than everyone just because you don't remember shit."

"Better? Do you have *any* idea how difficult—?"

"Oh, I get it," Eric sneers. "You're the victim. Poor little Seven! The whole fucking country is falling apart, but all you care about are your own problems. You're a fucking amnesiac. Get over it."

20
TAKE ME OUT

Crack! The bat splinters and a piece goes sailing toward the mound. The pitcher dives, making a narrow escape. The shortstop runs forward, grabs the ball with his bare hand and snaps it to first. The crowd cheers. Three outs, three-and-a-half innings down.

The judge should be sitting just a few rows in front of me in his usual spot, right on the foul line. But he's not. His four reserved seats are empty.

"Keep hanging on, everyone," David's voice says in my ear. "He'll be here."

"Excuse me again," rasps a once feminine voice. Big-boned Betty is back with her beer and hot dog. I stand up and press against my chair as tightly as I can. She squeezes through, takes back her seat next to me. "Thanks," she chokes.

It's funny. In one sense, this mission was obsessively well planned. I mean, like, I guess these Underground people don't have much actual training, but David seriously must have ripped this caper off of an espionage show. Hot dogs poisoned with laxative? Give me a fucking break. We should just snipe the bastard. I mean, okay, sure, maybe that would cause more of a scene. And yeah, we don't want to make trouble for ourselves—that's how you get arrested. But here's where the plan starts falling apart: the target isn't even here. The entire mission is based on the assumption that Judge James T. Farnsworth will be here, and he's not.

"Trade him!" Betty screams as if an ant just bit her in the rear.

The first guy up for the Hawks apparently just struck out on three pitches.

If the judge does show up, this mission has the potential to be pretty damn hilarious. I can't wait to see Ana in her outfit, putting on a show. And it's going to be great watching the judge run to the bathroom with his hand on his ass. Serves him right, the bastard.

I really wanted to be the one making the kill in this operation. But, that said, I'd rather be out here watching the game than sitting in the bathroom on a dirty toilet. If I didn't hate Eric so much, I'd almost feel bad. He's gotta be real anxious in there with all that farting, plopping and groaning.

●

Crack! The ball sails deep into the outfield...and into the mitt of the other team. Two outs, already? Everyone is booing, and the players are leaving the field. Must be three outs.

Good God. Where the fuck is this guy?

"Worthless!" shouts some dick behind me.

"Oh I absolutely hate Harvey Jenkins," says Betty, twisting her head around.

"He's been playing so awful!" laments the guy.

"And he's a jerk!" exclaims Betty. "I was down at spring training this year, and he was an absolute prick!"

"Really?" the guy makes the mistake of asking.

Here we go again.

"Oh yeah!" she gushes. "Me and my girlfriend went to a game a few months ago in Crystal Cay. They were playing the Jets, and you know how Duncan's on that team now?"

"Yeah, they were buddies, right?"

"Old college buddies! And pricks, the both of them!" Betty pauses, possibly to take a breath. "See, after the game, all the players generally go to this bar a few blocks from the stadium. Me and my friend went, and Jenkins and Duncan went together.

"So me and my friend are at the bar, and we're talking to some of the other players, getting their autographs, having a blast, and you know, we're wondering where Jenkins is. Finally we see him and he's on his goddamned cell phone!

"So I go up to him with my baseball—I was having everyone autograph my baseball—and I says to him real politely, 'Hi, my name is Betty. Could you please sign this for me?' And you know what he says?"

"What?"

"He doesn't say anything! He waves me off and turns around."

"He turned around?"

"He turned around! He just kept on talking on his goddamned cell phone with his ugly back in my face!"

"Huh," says the guy uncertainly.

"Can you believe it?"

Maybe it was an important phone call, I want to interject. But the last thing I need is to get on this bitch's nerves, so I perpetuate my stare across the field. Anyway, I'm on a mission. Sure Farnsworth isn't here yet, but still.

God, where the fuck is he?

●

Crack! The baseball sails over the shortstop's head and into center field. The stocky guy who hit it runs through first.

"Like, they really need to make some trades," says a dude in a backwards Hawks cap, sitting in front of me. "Like, this pitching is heinous! We don't even have an ace."

"Yeah, seriously," says his flannel-wearing friend.

"I mean, like, dude, trade fucking Garcia and a couple minor league players, get someone like Jones or O'Toole on the team."

"You really think the Rockets would trade Jones for Garcia?"

"Nah, I guess not. I think we could get O'Toole though, definitely."

"Yeah, probably."

Crack! The pill soars high into the night sky and lands somewhere in the upper decks. The boos are terrific. "You have to be fucking kidding me, Garcia!" Betty shreds what's left of my eardrums. I check for blood.

"God damn it, David," radios Eric. "What the fuck is going on?"

"He'll be here," says David. "Just hold on a little longer."

"God damn it!" steams Betty. "That's four to nothing already!"

"If he doesn't come soon, I'm going to have to make a new batch of hot dogs," mutters Ana.

"Just hold on," David says again.

I'm keeping my complaints to myself, but this really is starting to get ridiculous. It's the fifth inning. People aren't usually this late to games. But I just don't see the point in whining to David. I'm new to the team, anyway; I don't have experience with shit like this. I have to trust that he knows best. Anyway, I don't want to leave and have Farnsworth show up after all. I really want to see the son of a bitch pay for all the shit he did. Adrian, wherever he is, will be proud. In a way, his dad will be avenged.

"You know, kid," Betty says. She's leaning toward me, and I want to spray her sunburned arms with disinfectant. "You've been awful quiet tonight."

"Oh," I say with a start. "It's just..." What am I trying to say? "They're so bad..."

"Amen to that," she says, clapping a hand against her leg. "But it's not good to bottle up all that anger. Give 'em hell every now and then; you'll feel better."

"Either that or buy some more beer!" guffaws the guy behind us. He slaps my back. Betty cackles.

•

"Shit," the backwards-hat dude grumbles.

"What's the matter, man?" Flannel kid asks his apparently bummed out friend.

"I have that fucking Slammer song stuck in my head."

"What, 'Jackhammer'?" says flannel kid.

"Yeah."

"Love that song."

"Yeah, me too, but like, I've got the fucking chorus going in my head, except I can't think of the third line," the dude says.

"Oh shit," says his partner. "I hate when that happens."

"Do you remember it?" prods the dude.

"Shit, I don't know, man," says flannel boy. "What were the first two lines again?"

The crowd roars. Garcia just struck someone out. "That's more like it!" cries Betty. "Jenkins!" she squawks at the left fielder. "How many outs, ya jerk?!"

I rub my temples with the hope that it will help my headache. I guess this still isn't as bad as waiting in a toilet stall—Eric must really be freaking out. The judge hasn't even arrived at his seat. Eric's going to be waiting in there a good while longer.

"Seven," says Eric, speak of the devil. "Any sign of him?"

"Nope."

"What?" inquires Betty.

"What do you fucking mean, 'nope'?! David, what is this shit?!"

I turn to Betty. "Nothing, just talking to myself."

"Oh," she says after some hesitation.

David produces something like an ocean roar with one long, slow breath into his microphone. "Something's wrong," he says at last.

"What?" says Ana.

"We're going to abort," he says. "Meet back at the car. We're getting out of here."

That can only mean one thing: the judge isn't coming. What the fuck is going on?

"I'm going to get something to eat," I tell Betty.

"The hot dogs are fabulous," she says. "Don't eat too many though; they can give you bad gas."

•

We're on the highway. A news lady's blabbing away on the car radio, but no one's listening.

David clears his throat. "I'm not sure what happened," he says. "But we have to put this one behind us."

Eric moans, "I need to take a fucking shower—"

"Stop whining," says Ana. "I let you have shotgun, didn't I?"

A siren. I turn and see flashing red and blue lights. The Guard.

"Oh fucking hell!" yelps David, eyes burning through the rear-view mirror.

"Are you speeding?" snaps Ana.

"I don't fucking know! I don't think so!"

"They don't know who we—?" I ask.

"We haven't done anything," grumbles Eric. "And it's not illegal to carry a gun. We're fine. It's just another fucking hassle. This is the worst fucking night—"

"Wait, shut up!" David yelps, his fingers cranking up the radio.

"...will face execution for funding the Underground, a secret organization containing what top Guard officials have called 'the most dangerous pool of Heretics in the country.' In a statement released minutes ago, the President called the arrest of Young 'an extraordinary victory' for the newly formed Department of Purity."

"Oh my God," Ana whispers.

My head slams backward and the highway lights blur. We're swerving around a car, then a truck, then two more cars. I turn my head—the police car hasn't lost any ground. We cross two lanes and shoot down an exit ramp. Ana's leaning out the window with a gun. The Guard vehicle swerves back and forth a few times. Ana keeps firing.

Glass splashes over my neck. I duck while Ana leans in to take shots out the gaping hole in the back. Our pursuer squeals off the road, crashes into the railing. "I got him!" she yells. "Keep going!"

More sirens.

"Fuck!" screams Eric.

"Where are we go—?" I trail off.

"Fuck!"

"Everyone just shut the fuck up!" David bellows. "We're going to get through—"

Crack! The driver-side window explodes. David falls into the wheel.

Eric, soaked in red, squeals like a pig. We pick up more speed under our leader's dead weight. Eric bends for the wheel just in time to avoid an 18-wheeler.

"The ignition, Eric!" Ana shrieks. "The ignition!"

"What?!" he yells back. Ana flies forward, pulls the key out. The car slows. We coast off the road.

Eric shifts into park. He jumps out of the car, runs around to the driver side, pulls open the door, and tugs at David. "Seven, give me a hand!"

Cars and trucks whiz by. For an instant I see a little kid plastered against the window of a minivan. My ears prick up. The sirens are getting closer.

"He's not breathing! We have to get him out of the car!"

"Seven!" Ana pushes. "Move!"

Eric pulls open my door. I drop out and stagger toward the slumped David. Eric grabs at our leader's right shoulder. I grab his left arm. We start pulling. The siren gets louder.

David slides onto the asphalt. The siren is deafening.

•

"Get your hands up!" yells a Guard, leaping out of his vehicle. My arms rocket into the air. Eric dives into the blood-soaked driver's seat and the Guard sprints after him.

The soldier grabs Eric by the neck and tears him out and onto the pavement, next to David. My arms are wrenched down behind my back by a second officer. I fall and taste the road.

This is how it's going to end. I'm going to be dropped.

Eric gasps and groans. I shut my eyes.

"Halt!" someone new yells. My eyes open and take in a slowing black limo. It pulls over several yards in front of our car. A gray-haired man in a suit and driver's cap steps out. He jogs in our direction.

My Guard meets him halfway. They engage in muffled conversation; their stiff bodies block out the highway's halogen white.

Eric stops moving. His attacker snaps to his feet and aims his pistol up the highway. I follow his sights to Ana's back, sliding into the night.

Crack! Ana screams, stumbles. The shooter races after the falling body. The limo driver clears his throat and resumes dialogue with the Guard.

•

Ana, dead—or maybe just unconscious—is being pulled into the backseat of the cop car. David and Eric are still on the ground.

The Guard stares at me. He nods, and then looks over at his partner. "Hey!" he yells.

The other Guard slams the door on Ana and strolls back. "What's going on?"

"We're leaving this one," he says, pointing at me.

There's a click and my hands are free. "Help me with the other."

They move for Eric, grab a hand each and drag him to the car.

"Hey, Seven," says the limo driver, all smiles. "Follow me, please."

I don't move.

"You've got nothin' to worry about," he says. "You've done well. Please, come with me."

One of the Guard turns back and offers me a threatening look of reassurance. I don't have a choice.

I struggle to my feet, follow the driver to the limo. He pulls open the back door. "Come on in," a woman says.

I look inside.

"You?" I choke.

"Hi there," says Kira, grabbing at my collar. I fall into the car and she kisses my lips. "I've missed you."

The driver closes the door and disappears. The engine starts up and the limo slips into the smoky traffic.

"What's...what's going on?!" I sputter.

Kira strokes my hand and I get an eyeful of diamond sparkling on her finger.

"Don't worry," she says. "All your questions will be answered very soon. All you need to know right now is that the nightmare's over and you're going to be okay. You've done really well and I love you."

A nightmare. That's what this must be. Except, why can't I wake up? This has to be a dream. It has to be. I can't wake up!

"You're breathing pretty heavily, honey," she says. "Let me get you some water." She procures a plastic bottle and unscrews the top.

Why is she wearing a ring? She couldn't have gotten engaged

since I last saw her, could she? Is she married? Was she cheating on someone? God, shut up—that's not even important! I'm probably going to be killed within hours.

Oh my God. David and Ana might be dead. Oh my God.

"Where are they taking them?" I gasp finally, my eyes fixed out the back window.

"To the holding cells beneath the Capitol Tower," she says, folding my fingers around the water container. "They'll be questioned and then dropped."

I take a long, long gulp of the water. Kira looks delighted. She comes in close and gives me another passionate kiss. I pull back and take another look at the ring.

"I still love it," she says, beaming.

"Still?" I look up in disbelief. "It's... where did you get it from?"

"Aw, honey, I guess you wouldn't remember, huh?" She giggles. "You gave it to me."

21
ANNIHILATION

The leather sofa is soft, but I'm not comfortable. Kira—or Eve, as she now claims—squeezes my hand. She loves me. She says I'm engaged to her. I've been so desperate to see her since everything went wrong at the Red Lion. But not like this. Not here.

"What are we—?" My voice cracks. "What are we doing here?"

"The answer is on the way," she says, stroking my hair. It's not soothing. "Just relax. It will just be a little while longer, I promise."

I don't understand any of this. Why didn't the Guard take me? What does this all have to do with me? I keep trying to ask this girl, and she won't tell me a damn thing. All she does is look into my eyes, stroke and kiss me. It's what I thought I wanted and yet I'm so out of it—it's like I'm not even really here.

The knob shakes, but the door doesn't budge. The knob shakes again. "Dang door," complains a gruff voice on the other side. The man rattles it once more and finds success—and Claire's brother shuffles through.

"Welcome to the Capitol Tower, my boy, and congratulations—you've done well," George says. "Oh, and hello, Eve."

"Hello, sir."

I sip my water.

"I know, I know," he says. "This must all be a shock to you, but I'm going to explain everything. And then we'll get you all back to normal!"

I choke on the liquid. "Normal?" I cough.

My alleged fiancée pats my back. George continues.

"I believe you heard about the President's decision to up our anti-Heresy measures. Well, part of that program involved loosening a few restrictions we had on citizen surveillance. And another part involved the adoption of the absolute cutting edge in science!"

"Science?"

"Echolalia can be a side effect to surprise," George whispers to Eve with a wink. He looks back at me and booms: "That's where you come in. Your real name is Jonathan Wyle, and you are an Elite Guard—one of our very best! A few weeks ago, you volunteered to take part in an experimental mission to infiltrate the Underground and acquire vital information about how they operate, who's in charge..." George flaps his hand as if to swat a fly. "...and so forth."

"No, that's not possible," I say. "I don't remember any of that."

"Of course you don't—that's the idea. Despite what you may think at this point, the Guard does not underestimate the intelligence of the Underground. We've tried sending undercover agents in before and experienced *tremendous* failures. You need to be a certain kind of person to fit in with the Heretics. You have to have the same drive, the same anger. And you absolutely can't be a member of the Guard! I mean—you saw their database—they have ways of finding out your background. Those Heretics are smarter than you'd think!"

"Get to the point."

George sniffles. "Well, we figured a way around it. The problem was identity. The Underground figured out how to hijack our copious records, which means they can pretty easily pick the wolves from the sheep, so to speak. So, when we sent you, we erased your identity completely!"

George pauses, as if expecting a high five. "And it worked! They took you in as one of their own! And now thanks to you, we will be pure in a matter of weeks, maybe days!"

"Erased?" I laugh. "That's ridiculous. Why would I agree to that?"

"Well, no, not really erased," George mumbles. "I suppose 'Blocked' would be more...would be more accurate. We implanted a small microchip in your skull to suppress your memories—pretty cutting edge, really."

I rub my scalp closely, carefully. And I feel string—stitches. They might be telling the truth about me.

"But I have free will," I insist. "There'd be no way to ensure I'd ever do what you wanted."

"Oh, but we could push you in the right direction. Disguised as Kira, your fiancée Eve could easily exploit your attraction to her to forward the objectives of the mission. And you and I met on several occasions. I was the first person you came across, remember?"

I stroke the water bottle. "And that's why I had a map to the park?"

"Of course," claps George. "How would the mission go forward if you got lost at the very beginning?"

I crunch the plastic. "How'd you know what train I'd be on?"

"Oh!" George exclaims with a short laugh. "Well, that chip in your head—the one I told you about—that chip is more than a mere memory suppressant."

Suddenly, George falls into a coughing fit. Eve tears the water out of my fingers and passes it to George. He snatches it, throws his head back and chugs. Then he wipes his mouth and tosses the bottle at a wire wastebasket.

It misses wide and clatters against the floor. "Thank you, dear," he says. "Sorry, where was I?"

I grit my teeth. "You were saying the chip is more than a memory suppressant."

"Ah yes! Well, as I said, that chip employs the most—"

"—cutting edge in science," I sneer.

"Precisely," he laughs. "The chip contains audio recording, satellite GPS and wireless broadband capability. We effectively turned you into a tape recorder—everything you heard, we heard. To figure out what train you were on, all I had to do was watch and listen."

"It was very effective," oozes Eve.

"This is true!" Another laugh erupts from George's belly. "Considering you weren't going to report in yourself, it was the only option."

My eyes close. "But if you saw everything," I say, "how could you let your own nephew get murdered?"

"Adrian was a Heretic, simple as that," George says with a shrug. "I was very disappointed in the boy when I heard he still shared the theories of his father. And then he tried spreading his views to the public..."

"You mean, my conversation with—"

"You weren't the only one he talked to, but we never had concrete proof. Your mission represented an opportunity to change that," George says, suddenly smiling. "Adrian wasn't lying when he told you he was being watched. But he never would have guessed the camera was right in front of him."

"Oh my God," I whisper. It's my fault. They used me to spy on Adrian. If he hadn't been so open with me about his feelings toward the government—

"We've watched Adrian very carefully over the years. We knew he had attained contact information with the Underground. We just didn't know where he was hiding it.

"That's why I sent you to live at my sister Claire's place. Adrian is predictable. I knew he would befriend you and tell you what he knew if you provoked him properly. All you had to do was explain your unique perspective on things. Adrian has always been a trusting fool like that."

I killed him.

"How many of you have been watching me?"

"Jon, you're one of us, so we of course respected your privacy. Only your fiancée had access, though she of course reported everything directly to me." George swallows. "Oh, and on a somewhat related note, don't worry about Elite Agent Doug Smith or anyone else you killed. We can't hold any of those missteps against you, given the nature of your mission. There was no way you could have known."

"In fact, we've already taken care of that," Eve says.

"I saw," I growl. An image of the most recent TV execution flashes through my mind. That poor kid. "Walt—from the hostel, right?"

"Walt was a Heretic," George says simply. "We were going to get him, anyway. At least he's infamous, now."

"And the Smith kill did give you more reason to call the phone number," Eve chuckles. "I had thought it was going to take a lot of work on my part to convince you to do that." Her hand sifts through my hair. "Not that I wasn't looking forward to it."

"Yes, Smith's death was convenient in some ways," he agrees.

"But...the Guard didn't take us down until my third mission with the Underground. Wouldn't that be...isn't that, you know, counter-productive to anything you'd want me to be doing?"

"Not at all," beams George. "The information they acquired on the first two wild goose chases was outdated and unimportant. And besides, we needed them to trust you. Of course, we had no choice but to end it once we found out you were going after Judge Farnsworth—we couldn't have had that—but we'd learned enough by that point, anyhow."

I've hurt and betrayed so many. Adrian's dead. If David, Ana or Eric are still alive, they'll be dead soon. And the entire Underground will follow.

"But enough of this. Let's get your memory back, shall we?" George grins. "We're going to put you under and take the chip out. When you wake up, you'll be Jonathan Wyle again."

I don't like the sound of it. "Will I remember any of this?"

"Well—yes, in a way," George says. "But—but we've got a good psychiatrist lined up for you, my boy. So—in time, I mean— you shouldn't be dealing with any nasty mental artifacts."

No. I can't be one of them, I can't. I'm not like them.

George looks uncertainly at Eve. "It's a psychiatrist, right? Or was it a hypnotist?"

"Oh, um," Eve stammers. "I thought it was a psychologist, actually."

George considers. "Perhaps, the psychologist studied hypnosis. I think that was it. Or perhaps—"

"What if I don't want to go back?" I interrupt.

Eve's eyes widen. "What?"

"Oh my!" George hoots. "My dear Eve, do you see what's happened here? They've brainwashed him with their propaganda! He actually believes in the Underground! What an amusing side effect!"

"Brainwashed?" I laugh. "The Underground doesn't brainwash. The Guard brainwash. The Underground is change."

"My word, Jon! Spoken like a true automaton! Do you even know what the Underground is?"

I look away.

"Didn't it bother you at all to find out the Underground was led by the wealthiest man in the country?" George continues. "I mean, seriously, Jon, what does he of all people have to be angry about? Think about it! What does Daniel Alexander Young have to gain from overthrowing the society that's done nothing but make him rich?"

I don't answer.

"Control!" George goes red in the cheeks. "Say you had your revolution, and say it went off without a hitch! Who takes power, Jon? Who becomes lord and master, then?"

The window's not far away. How high off the ground are we?

"What are you—?" George laughs. "You're not thinking about running, are you, my boy?"

"My name isn't Jon," I growl.

"I'm aware that the character of Seven is all you know. But you are so much more. You have a wonderful, happy life! You're engaged to a beautiful girl, earn millions every year working for the government—you're damn good at what you do! It's fine to be afraid, my boy. But you have to trust us on this."

"It's not about being afraid, and it's not about trusting you," I say, clenching my fist. "I just want...I just want you to remove this damn microchip and let me get on with my life. I can't...I'm not going back."

"He doesn't mean that," Eve pleads.

"No, no, Seven means it," he says. "But we're not here to help

Seven. Seven doesn't have a choice. The decision is already made."

"I'll die before you erase me."

"Stop it!" cries Eve. "What about me? I love you."

"You love me?"

"Of course I do!"

"You exploited me, made me betray the few people in this country that have the right idea. And for what? To keep the citizens asleep while you invade their lives? Go to Hell!"

She pulls away. George places a hand on her shoulder and whispers into her ear.

I get a crazy idea. When Ana told me about the Underground rebels, she described them as "reporters doing their job." They search and collect incriminating information on the government, with the hope of one day exposing it for what it really is. The Guard used the chip to make me betray my friends. But now that I've got the full story, maybe I can use the chip to overthrow the Guard.

"Just tell me one more thing," I say. "The recorded audio—is it kept in the chip's memory…or the computers here?"

George looks up, befuddled. "Both. But we don't need the data anymore. The computers will be cleared, and the chip destroyed."

"Then I'm keeping the chip," I say.

George snorts. "You can't keep the chip. It's not your—"

A siren blares. The sound is deep and terrible.

"What's going on?" George asks us.

Eve, teary-eyed, grabs my hand and pulls me onto my feet. George reaches into a nearby drawer and procures a pistol. I fiddle with the door knob, finally get it open.

In the next room, people are running around in circles. A television set glares with pixilated jets and a blood red sky. A caption on the screen reads: ENEMY FIGHTERS SIGHTED OVER CAPITAL.

"What's going on?!" demands George, waving the gun.

People are screaming. People are crying. People are curled under tables.

"The war," whimpers Eve, white as a corpse. "It's come home."

22
DON'T LOOK BACK

"We've been hit!" Eve bawls. "They're targeting the Capitol Tower!"

The next tremor unearths George, sends the old man careening into a table. His gun goes flying. Eve squawks like a hen, swoops to his aid.

With the pair distracted, I dart for the weapon. Don't think they see me.

The television bleeds snow and screams static. I pick up the gun and turn for George and Eve.

My captors' fear-filled eyes meet. George mumbles something, but a heavy air raid siren suffocates the words.

"I—I don't know," Eve tells him. "But we've got—we've got good men with him. They'll get him out."

The fire door slams behind another cluster of escapees. George's mood turns profane: "Traitors!" he roars. "Someone help me! I'm your goddamned superior!" He shakes his head in disbelief.

Eve runs a hand over his forehead. "Sir, we have to get going."

"I know, I know," he says solemnly.

The girl's eyes flood into mine. "Honey, can you help me with him?" she cries. "I think he might have a sprain."

George gazes gloomily at the floor.

"No," I say, turning the gun on her.

"Jon?" Eve whimpers. "What are you doing? We have to get out of here."

"Tell me how to access the chip's memory."

"Be reasonable," says George, rubbing his leg. "You're not going to get far if we leave that thing in your head. If we don't remove the chip, you'll always be watched."

I take my best shot at an evil smile. "Not if there's no one to watch me," I hiss.

"But—" Eve starts.

"Give it to him," groans George. "There's no time."

Eve reaches into her pants pocket and pulls out a thin black stick. "Just put it in any computer and—"

I snag it.

"—enter the password, which is…" She bites her lip.

There's a crash, and the screaming gets louder.

"Yeah?" I yell.

"Hide and seek," she says.

My heart pounds, and I remember.

●

The leaves are everywhere, brown, yellow and red. Eve's soft black jacket disappears behind the tree. I run for it and trap her against the oak.

"You were supposed to count," she whispers.

Her hair is soft in my hand—softer than it looked. "I love you," I say.

Her fingernail runs down my chest and I shiver.

I drop to one knee.

"Jon, what are you—?"

"So, this is going to sound cliché, but you make me happier than anyone I've ever met," I say. "And the hardest—the hardest thing about this mission is going to be not having you by my side. I want—I want to make sure that, when it's all over, we'll never be apart again."

Her eyes are like oceans.

My hand opens. "Eve, will you marry me?"

●

"You don't have to kill me," Eve pleads. "That stick is the only way into your head. We didn't make copies. And—and—if you don't believe me, you can change the password to whatever you want."

I stare at my fiancée. Even in distress, she's the most beautiful girl I've ever seen.

"Please…"

"Why should I believe you?"

"Because I would never betray you," she cries. "Not even for the Guard!"

My eyes gravitate toward white magnet letters on the building directory by the door.

"Holding cells," I whisper.

"What?"

I'd almost forgotten: my friends—the ones I betrayed—are locked away in the Capitol dungeon.

"Eve," I choke, pulling back the weapon's safety. "I'm sorry it had to end up this way."

This is for Adrian.

I close my eyes and squeeze the trigger.

George gurgles his last breath. I turn away to join the pack pushing through the fire escape.

"Jon!" Eve screams. "Don't leave me!"

I don't look back.

•

Another explosion rocks the building, but this time it's accompanied by shrieking metal and a splash of granite. I take the steps two at a time, my feet barely caressing each plastic-coated platform.

This might be a pointless move. When I left the rebels on the highway, none of them were moving. David and Ana took bullets and Eric was beat to a pulp. But the soldiers loaded them into their car all the same.

There's a plug in the drain several steps down. Panicking Guard and government staffers are clustered like ants. It's the ground floor—everybody's destination but mine. I won't have to join the colony just yet.

"Holding cells," I breathe. Based on what I'd seen on television and what I'd heard about them from Adrian, the term is a misnomer. People that go down there don't get held—they get killed. The question is: how long do they have to wait? Maybe my friends didn't live long enough to see the Enemy tear their world asunder. But I can't leave them behind without knowing. I owe them that much, at least.

What if there are others? I mean, of course there will be others. It's fucking called the holding cells, not cell. But just saving Ana and Eric is risky enough. Unless there's an incredibly obvious way to spring the whole compound, I'm not going to have time. I'm not superhuman.

A muted boom shakes the building. A scream several flights up stabs through my heart like a dagger.

Oh God. What if I don't make it?

I press up against the wall to let by a Guard hurtling up the stairs. "What are you crazy?" he yells at me. The squeaky voice is unbefitting for a man with such broad shoulders. "We're all gonna die!"

He might be right. "So be it," I exhale. The descent continues.

I don't expect them to forgive me. My espionage may have been unwitting, but that doesn't change the fact that my entrance into David, Ana and Eric's world got them hurt, maybe killed. Not to mention the arrest of their leader, Daniel Alexander Young. God, I single-handedly unearthed and destroyed the Underground. No way Ana and Eric are going to take that well. But maybe I can try to make up for it.

●

The stairs end and suddenly a black door marked *Holding Cells* is in arm's reach. I push through the door and find something that looks more like a film set than a prison. A movie camera directs my attention to a stand I recognize instantly from TV: it's the spot where grinning reporters tally up the nation's executions.

My shoulders brush against the film equipment. I stop and gasp. Through the large window backdrop hangs Daniel Alexander Young, wearing the same suit he brought to church. They didn't put a bag over his head. His eyes bulge. His tongue droops.

A rapid pounding turns my head from the scene to a door on the other side of the room. A muffled scream gets my feet moving.

"Ana!" I yell.

"Seven!" she exclaims. "Get us out!"

The door knob doesn't budge. "It's locked!"

"What do you think you're doing?" sneers a stranger behind me. It's a Guard. His skin is bone white.

Where did he come from?

"The Enemy is bombing the city," I say calmly.

"I know, I know," he says, shaking his head. "It's safer down here. The bombs—the bombs can't reach us down here."

"Can you open this door? We have to get everyone out."

The Guard's stone eyes grow colder. "They're Heretics."

"What does it matter, anymore?"

"What does it matter, anymore?" he apes, cheeks reddening. "What does it matter, anymore?"

"Open the door."

"What does it matter, anymore?" he guffaws, reaching into his pocket. He pulls out a set of keys. "What does it matter, anymore?"

The door opens. Ana's shoulder is bandaged and bloody, but it's apparent she's had time to adjust her hair. Eric has two black eyes, chipped teeth and blood-crusted lips. He looks like a jack-o-lantern.

The cell isn't large. "Isn't there anyone else?" I ask.

"Turnover is high down here," states the Guard.

Ana's foot shoots into the soldier's crotch. He crumbles.

"David," I stammer at Eric. "Is he—?"

"Don't know," he says. "They took him."

"What's going on up there?" Ana prods.

"We're being attacked."

"Attacked," Eric echoes. He stumbles after his girlfriend.

Everything goes black. "The power!" screams Ana.

My eyes race back to the entrance and catch an orange exit sign burning on, apparently hooked to a backup generator. "Look," I say, grabbing Ana's hand. "We're going to get out."

"Eric, you see it?" she says.

"Yeah," he mumbles.

I stick my arms out like antennae and feel my way to the door.

"Thank you, Seven," Ana says. Eric grunts.

My hands find the door, get it open. The stairs are dimly lit by red backup power. We pump up the steps. Adrenaline dulls the pain.

I count the flights. "Just a little more," I say.

"Eric, we're going to make it!" Ana exclaims.

"Going to make it," he repeats.

Keep going, Seven. Just keep going.

We plow through a door labeled *Ground*. The hallway is dark, but I can see stars shining through an opening only several feet ahead. "Is everyone okay?" I ask, my breath heavy.

"We're okay," Ana affirms.

Suddenly we're out. Another blast strikes the Capitol Tower. This time, the shrieking is more severe. "Keep going!" I yell. "Don't look back!"

•

All that's left of the church is a fiery cavern, gated by a garbage dump of twisted metal and broken glass. The rubble spreads out about a block in each direction. We haven't seen the other cathedrals yet, but it wouldn't be much of a stretch to assume they look the same. The bombings weren't random. In its initial assault, the Enemy was clearly targeting state symbols.

The air raid siren cuts out. "Finally," grumbles Eric.

"Think they'll be back?" asks Ana.

"Those planes came from the ocean, and they turned back that way when they left," says Eric. "That means carriers can't be far offshore. This isn't a terrorist attack—it's war. I think the more important question right now would be if the sun is coming up anytime soon."

I press the light on my watch—Adrian's watch. "It's a little after midnight."

Eric emits a short snicker. "Long night," he says.

"This is where we part ways," I return.

Ana's eyes widen. "Sorry? What?"

I want to tell them about the chip, but I know I can't. The fact is that I betrayed these people. I don't know how I would even begin to explain who I was before and what's happened to me. The important thing is that I've saved them—they're alive. That's the best I could have hoped for.

"You guys should go on, get out of the city now," I say. "But I need a few more hours to take care of some unfinished business."

"Oh," Ana says. "Well, I mean, we can stay with you a little, but then, I guess I don't know how long we're going to want to stick around the city," she says, voice racing. "I mean, you heard Eric—the Enemy is going to be back. I'm not—I'm not sure we can wait for you. We've got to get out—"

"Don't wait for me. I'll figure a way out."

She looks at me for a long time. Finally she comes in for a hug.

"We owe you our lives," she says, squeezing.

"Please," I say, shaking my head. "I don't deserve it."

You don't know what I've done.

"Fine," she purrs. "Well, can we at least wish you good luck?"

"Yeah," I say, gazing at the smoking sky. "I suppose we all could use some of that."

•

The secret entrance to the Underground clicks into place behind me, and suddenly I'm submerged in black. I walk slowly, letting my hands trace the tunnel's cool walls. Finally, I reach the door, pull it open and flick on the lights.

Same old ugly hole, but no David, Ana or Eric.

The Guard's copies of my memory must be gone now, destroyed along with the Capitol Tower. Assuming George and Eve told me the truth, that means the only remaining evidence is in my head. But it's not going to do anyone any good there.

I switch on David's computer.

The Guard caught Daniel Alexander Young, but I refuse to believe the Underground went with him. These guys are smarter than that. HQ has still got to be out there somewhere, compiling a record of all the government's violations of civil liberty.

I stick the memory stick in the drive.

Maybe it won't matter. Maybe the Enemy's attack marks this fascist nation's end of days. But I don't believe it. Decades ago, the government used an attack on the Capitol to tighten their grip on the people. If the Guard can fend off the Enemy, they'll have an opportunity to make things worse. And even if they don't, there's no guarantee things will get better. Who knows what the Enemy is capable of doing.

The screen beckons me for a password. I type *hide and seek* and hit enter.

Connecting, says the computer. A photo of my face and the caption *Jonathan Wyle* appears. A menu to the right offers three options: *Watch*, *Copy* and *Exit*.

I select *Copy* and save everything onto the computer. Then I open a secure connection to HQ.

An email window pops up. In the subject line, I type *New Evidence -- Urgent*. In the body, I write: *Hope this helps!* Below that, I sign: *Your friend, Seven*.

I attach the file, lean back and take a deep breath.

When I send this, the Underground will know everything—who I am, what I did. What if they don't understand I'm trying to help? Guess that's just the price I pay for enlightenment.

I hit send and close the connection.

The End

ABOUT THE AUTHOR

 Adam Bender writes speculative fiction that explores modern-day political fears with a balance of action and romance.

Adam self-published his first novel, *We, The Watched*. His manuscript for the sequel, *Divided We Fall*, was a quarterfinalist in the 2013 Amazon Breakthrough Novel Awards, one of the top 100 novels selected in the sci-fi category. He has also written several short stories.

A journalist by day, Adam has reported extensively on technology and the international debate between personal privacy and national security. He is a senior journalist for *Computerworld*, *Techworld* and *CIO* in Sydney, Australia. He previously covered US politics on Capitol Hill for the esteemed Washington trade journal, *Communications Daily*. He has won journalism awards from the Society of Professional Journalists (SPJ) and the Specialized Information Publishers Association.

Adam maintains an active social media presence on Twitter (@WatchAdam) and Facebook (facebook.com/wethewatched). He also has a website and blog located at adambenderwrites.com.

He lives with his wife in Sydney.

DIVIDED WE FALL

The war has come home. The mission has failed. But all Eve wants is to get her Jon back.

Agent Eve Parker refuses to accept Jon's change of heart when he loses his memory and becomes a revolutionary known as Seven. Her mission is to stop him from overthrowing the President and the Headmaster of the Church. However, when Eve learns more about the President's plan to broaden citizen surveillance through a national ID program, she begins to question what she's always believed to be right.

Seven runs, but in his flight realizes that losing his memory may not have been enough to erase his feelings for Eve. Unable to escape his past, Seven determines that he must come to terms with the man he was if he ever wishes to win freedom.

Divided We Fall, the upcoming sequel to *We, The Watched*, was a quarterfinalist in the 2013 Amazon Breakthrough Novel Awards, one of the top 100 novels selected in the sci-fi category.

An independent reviewer from *Publishers Weekly* wrote that the story "raises interesting questions about the influence of propaganda on the construction of the self, the idea of true tabula rasa and the power of memory." In addition, "the central love story propels the narrative energetically."

Coming soon! Follow Adam's blog at adambenderwrites.com/blog for updates.

Made in the USA
Charleston, SC
01 June 2016